godless

Also by Pete Hautman

Sweetblood
Hole in the Sky
Mr. Was

godless

PETE HAUTMAN

Simon & Schuster Books for Young Readers

New York London Toronto Sydney

SIMON & SCHUSTER BOOKS FOR YOUNG READERS
An imprint of Simon & Schuster Children's Publishing Division
1230 Avenue of the Americas, New York, New York 10020
SIMON & SCHUSTER BOOKS FOR YOUNG READERS is a trademark of Simon &
Schuster, Inc.
Book design by Greg Stadnyk
The text for this book is set in Meridien.
Manufactured in the United States of America
10 9 8 7 6 5 4
Library of Congress Cataloging-in-Publication Data
Hautman, Pete, 1952–
Godless / Pete Hautman.— 1st ed.
p. cm.
Summary: When sixteen-year-old Jason Bock and his friends create
their own religion to worship the town's water tower, what started out
as a joke begins to take on a power of its own.
ISBN 0-689-86278-4
[1. Water towers—Fiction. 2. Religion—Fiction.] I. Title.
PZ7.H2887 Go 2004
[Fic]—dc21   2003010468

For those who would walk alone

Thank you to Scott Anderson, Leslie Harris,
Dorothy Hautman, and Sean McLoughlin,
for their water-tower stories

godless

IN THE BEGINNING WAS THE OCEAN. AND THE OCEAN WAS ALONE.

1

Getting punched hard in the face is a singular experience. I highly recommend it to anyone who is a little too cocky, obnoxious, or insensitive. I also recommend it to people who think they're smart enough to avoid getting punched in the face by the likes of Henry Stagg.

I was all those things the day Shin (real name: Peter Stephen Schinner) and I ran into Henry beneath the water tower. Henry was in the company of three lesser juvenile delinquents—Mitch Cosmo, Marsh Andrews, and Bobby Something-or-Other. None of the four were particularly dangerous one-on-one, but in a pack? That was different.

"Hey, Henry, how's it going?" I said, striving for the sort of gruff heartiness I imagined he might respect.

"Who's that? Is that Jay-boy and Schinner?" Henry

squinted ferociously, his face scrunched into a hard little knot. He was wearing his usual getup: beat-up cowboy boots, jeans, and a black T-shirt. "What're *you* guys doing here?"

"Just hangin' out," I said. I wasn't about to tell Henry what we were *really* doing there.

"With each other? You guys must be desperate," he said. Then he laughed. Bobby, Mitch, and Marsh all laughed too. The three stooges. Watching Henry as if he were the most fascinating thing they'd ever seen.

I have to admit, Henry Stagg is an interesting specimen. He's only about five-foot-five and scrawny as a wild cat, but Henry has *presence*. He's twitchy, cobra-quick, and wound up so tight you just know something has to give. Henry has a history of sudden, unprovoked violence. That makes him both dangerous and exciting company. Fortunately—or so I thought—Henry and I had always gotten along just fine. That might have had something to do with the fact that I'm twice his size. Also, I figured I could outthink him any day of the week.

"Could be worse," I said. "We could be hanging out with you guys." I laughed to make sure he knew I was kidding, which I wasn't.

Henry gave me a neutral scowl. "So how come you're hangin' out *here?*"

"We're working on a *science* project," Shin said in his Shinny voice. I groaned silently. I've gotten used to Shin's somewhat high-pitched, nasal voice, but it sends a guy like Henry right up the wall.

"A *science project?*" Henry said, lifting his voice to a quavering falsetto. "I thought fags were only interested in hairdressing and ballet."

"I'm not a *fag*," Shin said, his voice rising even higher. And I thought, *Uh-oh.*

"Not a *fag*?" Henry piped, raising his arms to display his knobby hands hanging slack from the ends of his wrists.

Shin, realizing that he was headed for trouble, crossed his arms over his notebook and went into his shell. More about that later. Henry capered in front of him, hopping from toe to toe, chanting, "I'm not a fag I'm not a fag I'm not a fag . . ." Shin just stood frozen, staring at the ground. Henry dropped his arms and walked up to him and stuck his face a few inches from Shin's and shouted, "Anybody home?"

Shin said nothing. Henry's jaw muscles flexed and the veins on his neck throbbed. Shin didn't even blink. When he went into his shell you couldn't pry him out if you stuck a firecracker in his ear. Not until he was ready.

Henry looked at me. "What's the matter with him?"

"Nothing," I said.

"Hit him," said Bobby. "Give him one."

The stooges laughed as if Bobby had said something witty.

Henry glared at them. Beneath it all, Henry had his rules. It wasn't his style to hit someone who was, say, unconscious. He wouldn't beat up a little kid, or an old lady—at least not without just cause. And he could sense that Shin, in his shell, was just as helpless.

"Push him over," Marsh suggested. "See if he, like, tips."

Henry put his palm against Shin's chest and gave a little test shove. Shin teetered, but his internal gyroscope kept him erect. Henry realized that a more aggressive push would topple Shin, but he decided not to do it.

"What's the matter with him?" Henry asked me again.

"He just gets that way sometimes."

Marsh said, "He must be, like, some kinda, like, freak."

"He's not a freak," I said, knowing that Shin was hearing everything.

Henry shifted his attention to me.

"You guys are both freaks. Look at you. How much do you weigh?"

"One ninety-four," I said, taking my standard thirty-pound deduction.

"I bet you weigh two hundred and fifty. You're huge."

I wanted to say something like, *To a Munchkin like you, everybody must look huge.* But I just looked back at him.

Then my head exploded.

At least that's what it felt like. I never saw the blow coming. His fist took me high on my left cheek, and the next instant I was laid out flat, wet grass soaking my back, staring up past Henry Stagg's florid knot of a face at the belly of the water tower, silver against blue sky. In the background I could hear the three stooges laughing, and I could taste blood where Henry's hard knuckles had smashed my cheek against my teeth, but mostly I was looking up at that enormous silver tank.

"It felt like an earthquake when you hit," Henry said, leaning over me. He was smiling happily, his face as relaxed as I'd ever seen it. Somehow I knew that he would not hit me again, at least not on that particular day. Whatever demon had been controlling him was temporarily sedated. We were safe.

But I have to explain myself. I have to explain why I didn't jump to my feet and pound the little creep into the ground. You might think it was because he had his friends to back him up, but that wasn't it. I'm not even sure they'd have done anything. The three stooges were bored and stupid and all they wanted was a little jolt of adrenaline. It didn't matter to them who got beat up— me, Henry, Shin, or any one of them.

The real reason I didn't jump all over Henry is quite simple, and I'm not ashamed to admit it: He scares the crap out of me.

I outweigh Henry Stagg by a good eighty pounds, I'm six inches taller, I'm coordinated, and I'm fast. I can grab a fly out of midair. I could take a guy like Henry any day of the week. But Henry has something I don't have.

Henry doesn't care what happens to Henry.

And that is why he can punch me in the face and get away with it.

Staring up at him, I could see it in his eyes. Henry didn't care. I could have thrown him against the tower's steel pillar and beat his head to a bloody pulp and that would have been okay with Henry. He'd just keep on swinging those hard, knobby fists, laying on the cuts and bruises and pain until I beat him unconscious, and he wouldn't care one bit. But I would. I'd care a lot. And that was Henry's power.

I respect power. Even in the hands of such as Henry Stagg.

Say you were walking down the street at night and you ran into me and Shin. Here is what you would see: two figures, dark and menacing. One is large-bodied, hulking, and neckless. That would be me. The other is thin, loose-jointed, with hair sticking out in every direction. That's Shin. If you are extremely observant, you will notice that Shin and I are the same height. Most people think I am taller, but I'm not. I'm just bigger.

Look closer now, as we come into the cone of light cast by a streetlamp. Shin is the one with the long fingers wrapped around a spiral-bound, nine-by-twelve-inch sketchbook. He is never without it. I'm the one with fat lips, freckles, and twelve dark hairs growing between my eyebrows. Like I'm half ape. Do you know who Orson Welles is? I look a little like Orson Welles. If you don't know who he is, then, never mind. Just think of me as the big, fat, pouty one.

We met in a computer workshop when we were ten years old. I was the smartest kid there, and Shin was the second smartest. That's according to a formula I devised based on knowledge of X-Men trivia, Game Boy performance, and the ability to lie with a straight face to the teachers. I was better at lying and X-Men, but Shin could out-game me.

Shin and I collaborated on a comic book that summer. We called it *Void*. It was about a bunch of guys fighting aliens on a planet where all the buildings were intelligent and all the plants had teeth. I drew the people, aliens, and plants. Shin would draw the buildings, machines, and cyborgs. My drawings were always full of drama and action; Shin was into the details.

Inevitably, we became best friends.

There are times, though, when I wish Shin was not who he is. His interest in invertebrates, for instance, can be embarrassing at times.

The day Henry Stagg flattened me beneath the water tower we were hunting snails, or "pods," as Shin likes to call them. That's short for gastropods, which is what you call slugs and snails if you are a science nerd like Shin. He had built himself a terrarium—he calls it a gastropodarium—and was looking to populate it with an assortment of slimers.

In case you're wondering, the reason we were looking for snails under the water tower (instead of someplace else) was because snails like moisture. It had been a dry summer, and the ground beneath the tower is always moist from the dripping tank. It wasn't really a science project. Shin just said that because he thinks science is sacred. He invokes science as if it were the name of God. Like it should be sacred to Henry, too.

Everything makes sense once you understand it.

Anyway, I was just glad that we'd run into Henry before we found any snails. That would have been bad. Henry probably would have made Shin eat them. Escargot, sushi style.

The reason I'm going on about Henry Stagg and snails is because that particular incident was a turning point in my life—one of those magic moments where suddenly the way you see the world changes forever. That's the other reason I didn't jump up and pound the crap out of the little monkey: I was busy having a religious experience.

I was flat on my back looking up past Henry at the silver, dripping bottom of the water tower tank, my head still scrambled, when it hit me just how important that tower was to St. Andrew Valley. It was the biggest thing in town. Water from that tower was piped to every home and business for miles around. The water connected all of us. It kept us alive.

That was when I came up with the idea of the water tower being God.

"Water is Life," I said, staring up at its silver magnificence.

Henry, shaking his head, walked away, saying, "You guys are both whacko."

2

BOCK!

I love to say my last name loud and hard and sharp.

BOCK!

It's a great name. Not great like Washington or Napoleon or Gates, but great in the sense that it is easy to remember and fun to say. Press your lips tight together and let the pressure build up until your throat is about to cramp, then let it fly.

BOCK!

Upon meeting a new supervillain or supermodel, I like to introduce myself as "Bock. J. Bock."

"Ah!" A tilt of the polished dome, a lumpy nose, cruel, thin lips peeling back from yellow teeth. "Goot eefening, Meestair Bock."

"Gruelmonger! I thought I recognized your wicked reek."

"Ha-ha. Most Amusing, Meestair Bock. Would you care for a Spot of our Delectable Grinslovakian Arsenic Brandy? Most Rare; most Deadly."

"I'll pass, if you don't mind. I am a bit tied up right now." Handcuffed to a chair.

"No, you muzz stay! We have a fascinating eefening planned for you."

"Sorry old chap, I really have to get back to my Aston-Martin." I dislocate several of my knuckles and slowly draw my right hand through the cuffs, disguising the excruciating pain with a sardonic smile.

"Your Aston-Martin? Tut-tut. You delude yourself—"

"—Jason Bock?" I look up, remember where I am, and scramble to my feet. "I'm here," I say.

The nurse beckons with her clipboard and I follow her out of the waiting room and down the hall.

My mother is convinced that I am suffering from some exotic and possibly terminal disease. At one time she was convinced that it was sleeping sickness, but Dr. Hellman talked her out of that. No tse-tse flies on this continent. Then she decided it had to be mononucleosis, but a blood test disproved that theory. Now she thinks I have something called narcolepsy. All this due to the fact that I love to sleep. I'm like a cat. I could sleep twenty hours a day. But, of course, she won't let me.

Dr. Hellman regards me wearily. "Jason, I understand that you are still having a sleeping problem."

I shrug. "My mom made the appointment."

Hellman sighs and looks over my chart. "Yes, I see she called and asked that we test you for narcolepsy." He smiles. "You are still spending a lot of time in bed?"

"Not more than twelve or thirteen hours a night."

"I see. Do you ever fall asleep in class?"

"School's out for the summer."

"Do you ever fall asleep in the middle of the day?"

"Every now and then. Like in the afternoon."

"Do you ever fall asleep suddenly at inappropriate times? Like while you're eating dinner?"

"No."

"Have you ever fallen asleep while driving?"

"I don't get my permit till October."

"I see. Of course." He looks at me. "What happened to your face?"

I reach up and touch the tender bruise left by Henry Stagg's fist. "I ran into a door."

"I see. Do you ever fall asleep while you are involved in an activity that interests you?"

"No. Unless I'm reading in bed. Sometimes I fall asleep even when I'm reading a good book."

"Do you ever fall asleep when you're not in bed?"

"Sometimes I lie down on the couch."

"Do you think that you have a sleeping disorder?"

"What do you mean?"

"Is your sleeping a problem for you? Does it prevent you from doing things you want to do? Does it affect your schoolwork?"

"Not really."

Hellman nods and makes a note.

"Jason, I could refer you to the Sleep Disorders Clinic at the university. It would cost you several hundred dollars, perhaps more, which might or might not be covered by your parents' insurance. You would probably have to stay there for a few days or nights while they monitored your sleep activity. Would you be interested in doing that?"

"Not really."

"The fact is, Jason, I don't think you have a problem."

"I never thought I did."

"Perhaps I should talk to your mother again."

"I guess so."

My mother's specialty is diagnosing rare diseases in other people. Not that she ever went to medical school. She has this enormous book describing every illness known to man, from nail fungus to cancer of the eyeball. She reads it the way some people read the Bible.

A few months ago my dad hit himself on the thumb with a hammer. Most people would see a swollen thumb requiring an ice pack and a Band-Aid. Mom saw it as an early sign of cerebral palsy. For weeks, she watched his every move, recording any sign of clumsiness. Dad moved through the house like a ballerina on eggs, doing everything he could to prove that he wasn't losing control of his limbs. Finally, to his relief, she lost interest in his case and began to focus on my sleeping habits.

Have I mentioned that my mom's nuts?

✳   ✳   ✳

Naturally, she zeroes in on my bruised jaw immediately.

"Oh my god, Jason, what *happened*?"

"Nothing."

"You have a *bruise* on your cheek!"

"I ran into a tree branch."

"What were you doing running into trees?"

"It was an accident, Mom."

"Are you feeling all right? What did Dr. Hellman say?"

He says you're a crazy woman, Mom. I don't really say that. I say, "He says I'm fine."

"Were you knocked unconscious when you ran into the tree?"

"No. I'm fine. And I don't have narcolepsy either."

"Oh, dear." She looks at me, touching her fingers to her lips. "I wonder what it could be?"

STILL, THE OCEAN WAS ALONE IN TIME, AND TIME WAS ENDLESS, AND SO THE OCEAN DREW IN UPON ITSELF AND BECAME FINITE, A WRITHING BALL OF WATER AND FOAM SURROUNDED BY NOTHINGNESS. AND THE OCEAN PASSED THROUGH TIME AND SPACE. BUT THE OCEAN WAS STILL ALONE.

3

While my mother is obsessed with my physical well-being, my father frets over my soul. Every Sunday, without fail, he drags me to mass at the Church of the Good Shepherd. In my opinion, he's a borderline religious fanatic.

A couple of months ago I made the mistake of leaving one of my drawings face-up on my desk. It was a picture of Bustella, the Sirian Goddess of Techno War. Bustella is very busty, and at times her clothing doesn't exactly stay on her body. In fact, in the drawing that my dad saw sitting on my desk, she was wearing nothing but a scabbard for her sword.

Next thing I knew he'd signed me up for Teen Power Outreach, better known as TPO, a weekly brainwashing session for teenagers held every Thursday night in the church basement.

My father believes in brainwashing. He's a lawyer. He thinks you can argue anybody into anything.

The head brainwasher is a car salesman named Allan Anderson, who insists we call him Just Al. Or maybe he meant we should *just* call him *Al*, but the first meeting I went to I called him Just Al and it stuck. Too bad for Just Al.

Just Al likes to start off every meeting with a prayer he made up. It goes something like this: "Dear Lord, Al Anderson here. Just wanted to say thanks for giving me another day here on planet Earth, and for getting every one of these kids here safely. We appreciate it, Lord. You're one heck of a guy."

The first time I heard Just Al deliver his prayer I must admit I was mildly amused, but now that I've heard it eight or nine times I'm pretty sick of it.

The purported idea of TPO is to give kids a chance to talk openly and honestly about God, religion, and Catholicism. But there is also a secret agenda to turn us all into monks and nuns, at least in terms of our relations with the opposite sex. Naked goddesses with big boobs have no place in TPO. Abstinence is one of Just Al's favorite themes.

Mostly, though, the meetings are just a bunch of pointless yakking. I try to keep myself interested by messing with Just Al's head. Here's an example:

Brianna: But, like, I mean, aren't there, like, people, like, starving to death and stuff? How can you, like, go to church and buy shoes you don't need and stuff when people are dying because they can't get enough to eat?

Just Al: It won't do anybody any good for *you* to starve. Catholic missions feed thousands of hungry people every year.

Magda: My aunt is Buddhist, and she works at the homeless shelter downtown. They feed people, too.

Just Al: Yes, but that shelter was founded by a Catholic priest.

Magda: Can you be Buddhist and Catholic at the same time?

Brianna: I don't *think* so.

Magda: How come only men can be priests? I mean, who wants to be a nun?

Me: I'd like to be a nun.

Magda: (laughs)

Brianna: You are so lame, Jason.

Me: No, really. You get to wear that cool thing on your head.

Brianna: Shut *up*.

Just Al: The priesthood is the oldest office known to man. Two thousand years ago they didn't have presidents or congressmen, but they had priests.

Me: So, how do priests breed if they can't have sex? Do they send out buds like amoebas?

Just Al: Ha-ha.

See what I mean? No matter what we talk about, Just Al always brings it back to how great the church is. And as for that bit about presidents and priests, well, that just gives you a measure of Just Al's intellectual depth. The man's a *car* salesman!

This Thursday's TPO meeting gets mired in a discussion of pedophile priests. The subject makes Just Al vastly uncomfortable. Normally I would enjoy his agonies of embarrassment, but I am thinking about water towers. I'd have just sat there quietly until the meeting was over, but Just Al notices me drifting off and tries to rope me into the discussion.

"Jason, what do you think about what Magda just said?" he asks me.

"I don't know." I look at Magda. Magda Price is what my grandmother would call "cute as a button," whatever that means. She has long, dark hair that is not quite curly but not straight either, big brown eyes to match, and lips you can't not look at. The only thing wrong with her is she's kind of small. Not Munchkin small, but close. Definitely too small to be interested in a hulking, neckless creature such as myself. "What did you just say?" I ask her.

"I wondered if God gives priests who commit mortal sins a second chance."

"I don't believe in God," I say.

This is not news. I've been telling them I'm an agnostic-going-on-atheist for several months now.

Just Al should know better, but he doesn't let it go. "So you've told us, Jason, but assume for a moment that you are wrong."

"Then I burn in hell for all eternity."

"So what *do* you believe in?" Magda asks.

"Actually, I worship a different god."

Just Al is giving me a nervous sort of look. "And what god would that be?" he asks.

"The Ten-legged One." I am making this up as I go along.

Brianna jumps in with her usual incisive comment: "You are so lame, Jason."

Just Al says, "Jason . . . you really shouldn't joke about such things . . ."

"Who's joking? I'm a member of the Church of the Ten-legged God."

They are all staring at me. Just Al doesn't have a clue what to do.

After a few seconds, Magda asks, "Do they let women be priests in the Ten-legged church?"

"The Ten-legged One has yet to address that particular issue."

After that, I refuse to speak further of the Ten-legged One—mostly because I don't know anything. I only brought it up to rattle Just Al. But the more I think about it, the more I like it. Why mess around with Catholicism when you can have your own customized religion? All you need is a disciple or two. And a god.

THE OCEAN CREATED LAND, SO THAT IT DID NOT HAVE ALWAYS TO BE WITH ITSELF. AND IT CAST OFF FIERY BITS OF ITSELF TO LIGHT THE SKY, AND IT CREATED WIND, AND IT FILLED ITSELF WITH TINY NODES OF ENERGY CALLED LIFE. AND STILL IT PASSED THROUGH TIME AND SPACE, BUT NOW IT WAS NOT SO ALONE.

4

Think about it: What is the source of all life? Water. Where does water come from? Water towers. What is the tallest structure in most towns? The water tower. What makes more sense—to worship a water tower or to worship an invisible, impalpable, formless entity that no one has seen since Moses. And all he actually *saw* was a burning bush.

I explain this to Shin, who stops walking and stares back at me as if my nose has turned into a tentacle.

"You're saying the water tower is God?"

"*Think* about it," I say.

Shin thinks about it.

"Prove me wrong," I say.

He gives it some more thought. "Suppose that what you say is true. Then are all water towers gods?"

"I'm not sure. I guess they must be. Some are lesser gods, though."

Shin nods his head slowly. "I like it." He starts walking again. We are on our way to Bassett Creek to hunt pods. Shin has added a new wing to his gastropodarium and is seeking new tenants. He says, "It makes sense, doesn't it? I mean, do we really *need* water towers?"

"People used to get along just fine without them," I say. "The Indians didn't need water towers."

"I wonder why they have manifested themselves now, after all these thousands of years."

"It must be some sort of sacred mystery."

"Maybe they're from another galaxy," Shin says.

"You mean like alien invaders?"

"Yeah. I used to think the water tower was a spaceship."

Now it is my turn to gape at him. "You did?"

"Sure. When I was a kid. I figured they were just waiting for the right moment to beam me aboard and take off."

"You really thought that?" I always knew Shin was weird, but he'd never talked to me about water towers being spaceships.

"Only till I was about ten. I figured they were stealing our water. And they'd have to take me when they left because I was on to them. The part I could never figure out was if they'd take off with their legs, or if just the tank would go, leaving the legs behind. I was kind of leaning toward them taking off legs and all. So that they'd have something to land on. Maybe the legs would retract into the tank."

"What about the central pipe?"

"You mean the sucker upper?"

"Yeah. The thing in the middle."

"That would retract too."

I give that a moment's thought. "They'd have to have a pretty powerful drive to take off with all that water aboard."

"Antigravity. And of course they'd use the water itself for fuel. Nuclear fusion."

"Of course."

"Of course."

"Of course."

"Of course."

I stop walking, because to continue would put me up to my waist in the rushing waters of Bassett Creek.

"Here we are. Now what?"

Hunting the Wild Gastropod: A Primer

1. Find a place both wet and rank with lots of decaying vegetation available.
2. Crawl around on your hands and knees and look for slime trails.
3. Avoid poison ivy, stinging nettles, biting insects, and snakes while doing so.
4. Upon locating pod, place in plastic container with some rotten leaves or whatever from the area where you found it.

5. Record details surrounding the capture: time
   of day, type of soil and plant matter,
   temperature and humidity, and pod behavior.

I am no great pod hunter, but on this day I manage to come up with a large slimer of a variety never before seen by pod god Shin. This particular snail has a light brown shell, a pale body, and black eye stalks.

The pod god is suitably impressed.

"I think it's a white-lipped snail," he says.

"Snails have lips?"

"The lip of the shell. See how it's kind of whitish?"

"Oh." It doesn't look all that white to me, but I don't argue.

"I didn't think we had any white-lips here. What was it doing?" he asks.

"Clinging."

"Clinging to what?"

"Rotting bark."

Shin places the white-lipped pod in his collection jar and makes a note in his sketchbook. Later he will make a careful drawing of the snail in its natural habitat.

I was the one who got him started on this gastropod kick. One day two summers ago I found a particularly large pond snail—it was almost three inches long—and showed it to Shin. "Wouldn't it be cool," I said, "to have a snail farm?" Next thing I knew, Shin had built himself a gastropodarium. Now Shin is the snail expert, and I just go along for the ride.

Aside from one small snapping turtle and a dead snake, we find no other cold-blooded creatures of interest at Bassett Creek.

Back at Shin's, we introduce the white-lip to his new neighbors, who do not so much as extend an eyestalk in greeting.

"Not very friendly," I say.

"Pods are not known for their exuberance," says Shin as he sprinkles a tablespoon of cornmeal into the gastropodarium. Snails like cornmeal.

Shin's gastropodarium is quite impressive. He started with a six-foot-long aquarium he found at a garage sale. The aquarium was no good for fish because it leaked, so he got it for five dollars, hauled it home on his wagon, and turned it into a snail paradise.

At one end of the gastropodarium is a small pond with algae and swamp grasses growing in it. A big brown pond snail—the one I found two years ago—still lives there, spending most of its time clinging motionless to a rotting cattail stalk.

At the edge of the pond, the land rises to become a rocky, mossy, leafy hillside, home to four or five types of land snail. Some of the smaller snails like to hang out in an old whisky bottle that lies near the shore. Others prefer the high ground, scavenging among the decomposing leaves that litter the hillside. A partially buried fox skull juts from the rocks near the top of the hill, its sharp white teeth framing the entrance to a cave, the source of a small stream that trickles down the hill to the pond. Somewhere in the tumble of rocks and dead leaves and earth, Shin has concealed a small recirculating pump.

Shin does nothing halfway. The gastropodarium is its own reality, a universe of gastropods within four glass walls. Have I mentioned that Shin is obsessive? When we were making comics together, he'd spend hours with an ultra-fine-tip technical pen drawing tiny rivets on his cyborgs. You almost needed a magnifying glass to see them. As for the snails, I have known Shin to spend hours with his forehead pressed to the glass, watching them. He says that to really understand something, you have to become whatever it is you are studying. He says he knows exactly how it feels to be a snail.

"You have to get to the point where you really believe you're a snail," he once said to me. "If you don't believe in your own snailness, you'll never understand them."

That's fine with me. I don't really want to know how it feels to crawl along a trail of my own slime.

"You know, it makes sense what you were saying about the water tower," Shin says as he adds fresh water to the snail pond.

"What did I say?"

"That I can't prove you wrong. I mean, you can't prove a negative, right? Like, you can't prove that God doesn't exist, and you can't prove that the water tower isn't God. Besides, when you get right down to it, it's a matter of relativity."

"It is?" I don't always follow Shin's logic.

"Sure. God is relative. As far as the pods are concerned, *I'm* God."

"Yeah, but a pod has a brain the size of a poppyseed."

"Doesn't matter. From the pods' point of view, I *am* God. They look up and I am this great shadowy figure—pods don't see much beyond light and dark. I am like a cloud that comes and goes. I provide their food and water. I control the temperature, the light, everything. I am the Pod God." He smiles down at his subjects. "You know what makes us different from them?"

"Aside from the fact that they're snails, and we're a couple of snail-collecting nerds?"

"We have the ability to quantify."

"Oh, yeah, I was just gonna say that," I said. Of course, I have no idea what he's talking about.

I am standing at the exact spot where Henry Stagg punched me in the face, watching Shin measure the distances between the ten legs of God with a yellow tape measure. Each leg is an enormous I-beam welded to a four-foot-square metal slab, which is bolted to a concrete base. The bolts are as big around as my wrists; the concrete base is set deep into the earth. I wonder why. You would think that the weight of all that water would be enough to hold it down, even in a storm.

The body of the Ten-legged One—I guess you'd call it the tank—looks like a giant silver M&M candy, only thicker. And instead of M&M, the letters wrapping around its side spell out ST. ANDREW VALLEY in black block letters ten or twelve feet high. How much water does it hold? Enough to fill every bathtub and swimming pool for miles around. Enough to water all the lawns, to wash all the cars, to power tens of thousands of toilet flushes.

The tower stands in the center of a grassy area, about 150 feet across, near the center of town. It's the tallest structure in sight. You can see it from just about any-where in St. Andrew Valley.

Shin is now measuring the circumference of the cen-tral column, the giant pipe that drops from the belly of the tank into the earth. I have not yet asked him why he is doing all this measuring. Sometimes it is more inter-esting just to sit back and watch.

A tight spiral of narrow metal treads wraps around the column. The staircase starts about fifteen feet above the ground. It winds around the column, circling it three times, to a point just below the bottom of the tank. From there, a catwalk leads out from the column to one of the legs, then a ladder ascends to a second catwalk wrapping around the perimeter of the tank like a belt around its middle, just under the ST. ANDREW VALLEY letters. Yet another ladder rises from the upper catwalk and follows the curve of the tank up to the top. I wonder what is up there, at its highest point.

Now Shin is walking away from the column with big, goofy-looking steps. As he passes me I hear him counting.

". . . thirty-four, thirty-five, thirty-six . . ."

He stops at the count of thirty-nine. He looks up at the tower, squinting into the sun and writes something in his notebook.

I can't stand it anymore.

"What are you *doing*?" I ask.

"Applying the principles of trigonometry." He hands me the tape measure. "Measure my shadow."

Shin's shadow is three-feet-four inches long. He records this fact in his notebook.

"You going to tell me what you're doing?"

"Quantifying," he says.

"Quantifying what?"

"God."

A ND THE OCEAN WATCHED AS ITS CREATIONS CHANGED, AS RIVULETS BECAME RIVERS, AS HILLOCKS GREW TO MOUNTAINS, AS FISSURES OPENED, AS THE FLOATING LIFE-UNITS BEGAN TO SWIM, TO CRAWL, TO FLY.

5

Dan Grant is my ordinary friend. Everybody should have at least one ordinary friend, and Dan is as ordinary as they come. He is so ordinary that most people have to meet him six or seven times before they remember his name.

Even the way he looks is ordinary. One time for a computer project I scanned a whole bunch of student photos from the yearbook, then used a graphics program to morph them into a single face. What I got looked like a slightly fuzzy version of Dan Grant. When I showed the picture to Dan, he didn't see the resemblance. But everybody else did.

In addition to being exceedingly ordinary, Dan is also a P.K., which stands for Preacher's Kid. His father, Reverend Andrew Grant, is the minister at Calvary

Lutheran Church. Naturally, the Reverend Grant expects his only son to follow in his hallowed footsteps. Dan would rather be a firefighter. No kidding. He's wanted to fight fires since before kindergarten.

I am playing ping-pong with Dan in his basement the day I decide to invite him to join Shin and me in our exploration of the Ineffable and Glorious Mystery of the Ten-legged One.

I am seven points ahead when I bring it up. The reason I am seven points ahead is because I have a psychological advantage over Dan, even though he is a better ping-pongist. He can't beat me. Here's how it works. First, I am bigger than him. Second, the first few times I hit the ball, I smack it as hard as I can, right at his face. Now you might think that getting hit by a little ping-pong ball wouldn't hurt, but you would be wrong. The very first shot I connected with Dan's forehead. He still has a red spot where it hit. And now, every time I hit the ball, he flinches.

That is what you call *technique*.

Between flinches, seven points ahead, I ask Dan if he has been saved.

"Saved from what?" he asks.

"Ignorance, dehydration, hellfire and damnation."

Dan thinks for a moment. It is one of his most irritating habits. Ask him his name and he takes a few seconds to consider his response.

"Yes," he says.

"Yes, what?"

"I've been saved from all three. School saved me from ignorance, Mountain Dew saved me from dehydration, and my father saved me from hellfire and damnation. At least I think he thinks I think he did."

"How did he put out the hellfire?"

"Huh?"

"How did he put out the fire?"

"He . . . what are you talking about?"

"What's the most important element on earth?"

"I don't . . . ah . . . oxygen?"

"Wrong. It's water."

"Water isn't an element. It's a compound."

"Earth, air, fire, and water. Those are the four elements, according to the ancient Greeks."

Dan stares at me, blinking. We've been arguing for ten years and he hasn't won one yet.

"What's your point?" he asks.

"Shin and I have a new religion," I tell him. "The Church of the Ten-legged God."

Dan comes off as such a straight-shooter that most people would be surprised to know how crazy he can be. For instance (very few people know this), he likes to chew aspirin. He says he likes the way it feels on his tongue. Maybe Dan isn't so ordinary after all.

He says, "What is it? Like, a cult?"

"Better than a cult. You don't have to dress weird or anything. No church on Sunday. And it's free."

"I like free. How many people do you have so far?"

"Three, if you join. I'm Founder and Head Kahuna.

Shin is First Keeper of the Sacred Text. We'd like you to be First Acolyte Exaltus."

"What does that mean?"

"I have no idea."

"Do we get to sacrifice virgins?"

"Possibly. Much remains to be decided. You're coming in on the ground floor."

"So why does this god need so many legs?"

"I don't know. Should we go ask him?"

A few minutes later Dan and I approach the Ten-legged One, looking up at its swollen belly. Shin is waiting for us. He is lying flat on his back on the grass with his mouth open.

"Is he okay?" Dan asks.

"I'm fine," says Shin.

"What are you doing?"

"Trying to catch a drop of Holy Water." Just as he speaks, a large drop hits his cheek. Shin closes his eyes and smiles and says, "Ahhhh."

"It's one of our sacraments," I explain.

"What are the others?"

"Giving Thanks to the Tower—that's where we bow in the direction of the Ten-legged One three times a day. And the Sacred Washing of the Hands. We do that before meals. The Flushing of the Toilet. We're working on more."

Dan crumples his brow, then says, "How about the Daily Immersion?"

"Would that be a bath, or swimming?"

"Either."

"I like it."

Dan looks up at the tower, then at Shin, then turns to me. "My dad would totally freak. Count me in, Kahuna."

Just then, Shin lets out a startled squawk. An exceptionally large water drop has hit him square on the forehead. But it's not just water. He sits up and wipes it away and stares at the glop dripping from his fingers. It looks like snot, or slime. My first thought is that a bird crapped on him, but then we hear laughter from above. We all look up and see a grinning red face hanging over the edge of the lower catwalk, 120 feet above us.

"Gotcha!" shouts the face.

It's Henry Stagg.

> FOR THREE BILLION YEARS THE OCEAN WATCHED, CONTENT, AS THE WORLD EVOLVED. IT WATCHED THE RISE AND FALL OF THE DINOSAURS, THE RISE OF THE MAMMALIANS, THE CETACEANS' RETURN TO THE SEA, THE MIGRATION OF THE CONTINENTS.

6

Father Haynes, a thousand years old at least, is standing in the pulpit delivering one of his famous sermons on selflessness. His voice rises and falls like the sound of a crop duster passing back and forth over a field, spraying us with words. I've endured this sermon before. It goes on for nearly half an hour, but the message is simple: Give more money to the church.

I could use some money, too, for necessities such as game discs and french fries and size-thirteen Nikes. Maybe I should collect dues from the congregation of the Church of the Ten-legged God.

I look to my left, at my father. His lips and jaw are set in a determinedly attentive mask, but his eyes are drooping. I'm not the only one who's heard this sermon before. I lean forward and look past him at my mother, hands folded neatly in her lap, a worried smile on her pink-lipsticked lips. Probably thinking about all the germs floating around the church. Influenza, hanta virus, ebola, bubonic plague . . .

Do they really think that attending mass will make them better, or happier, or save them from an eternity of hellfire? Maybe they do. But there are something like ten thousand religions in the world. What makes them think that they happen to have been born into the right one? I have asked this question several times. So far, I haven't heard a good answer. Better to start your own religion, I think. That way you get to be your own pope.

I'm well on my way. I have a god, I have sacraments, and I have two converts—plus myself. But the Church of the Ten-legged God (CTG for short) still needs one more thing: a set of rules, or commandments. I wonder what sort of commandments the Ten-legged One might hand down. I'll have to make some up.

Father Haynes has shifted gears and is now talking about respect for the sanctity of the church. I think he's upset because a few weeks ago he found some chewing gum stuck to the bottom of one of the pews. I wonder how he would feel about spit, and I think about Henry Stagg.

Nobody likes being spat on. As Shin disgustedly wiped his face clean with his shirttail, Henry descended the spiral staircase. Watching him trot confidently down the perforated metal steps, I couldn't help imagining that the Ten-legged One was sending an emissary down to speak with us, like God sending Jesus to Earth, only he turns out to be Adolf Hitler. When Henry ran out of staircase, still fifteen feet above us, he sat down on the bottom landing and dangled his cowboy boots over our heads.

"What are you guys doing?" he asked.

I was not about to tell Henry that we were there to worship the water tower.

"How'd you get up there?" I asked.

"I flew," Henry said.

"Yeah, right."

Henry shrugged. I looked around. No ladders, no ropes. No way he could have jumped high enough to reach that bottom rung.

Shin said, "You're not supposed to be up there."

Henry laughed.

"How are you gonna get down?" Dan asked.

"Why would I want to get down?"

"You have to come down *sometime.*"

"I don't . . . uh-oh. The law." Henry pushed himself off. For a moment he hung with both hands gripping the bottom step, his feet still about eight feet off the ground, then he dropped, hitting feet first, the heels of his boots punching into the soft ground.

"See? No problem."

A few seconds later a squad car pulled up to the grassy apron. Gerry Kramer, one of St. Andrew Valley's oldest and grayest cops, got out of the car and walked up to us, shaking his head.

"You kids . . . is that Henry Stagg? I thought we talked about this, Henry."

"Talked about what?" Henry put on his *Who me?* face.

Kramer wasn't buying it. Henry trying to act innocent is like a wolverine trying to act cuddly.

"Henry, Henry, Henry . . . what are we gonna do with you?"

"I don't know what you're talking about," Henry said, trying to hold back a grin.

Kramer stared until Henry lowered his eyes. "I don't need any more of these nuisance calls, Henry. Next time I get a kid-on-the-water-tower call, you're going downtown."

"I wasn't *on* the water tower, officer. Did you *see* me?"

"No, I didn't, but that doesn't change the facts. You were seen. I know it was you up there."

"So how did I get up there? You think I flew?"

Kramer shook his head, as perplexed as the rest of us. "You got up there somehow."

"I guess I musta flew."

"Well, you can fly home right now. I don't want to see you—" He crossed his thick arms and looked at the rest of us. "—*any* of you around here again. You hear me?"

"Yes, sir," said Dan. Dan is terrified of authority figures.

We edged away, feeling Kramer's hard eyes on our backs. As soon as we were out of earshot, Henry said, "What an asshole."

"He's just doing his job," Dan said.

"Yeah, well he can shove it." We reached the sidewalk and continued walking up Louisiana Avenue. It felt strange to be walking beside Henry Stagg, but the confrontation with the law somehow bound us together.

"Did he catch you up there before?" I asked.

"Just once. A couple weeks ago."

"What were you doing up there?" Dan asked.

"I like it. You can see forever. You can see the school. I can see my house."

"You ever go all the way to the top?" Shin asked.

"Sure, all the time."

"What's up there?"

"All kinds of stuff."

"Like what?"

"You should check it out, Schinner."

"You're not supposed to."

"Well then, you'll never know, will you?"

Shin shook his head and drew his mouth into a knot.

"So how *did* you get up?" I asked.

"Like I said, I flew."

Father Haynes ends his tedious sermon and launches into the Nicene Creed. I know all the parts of the mass. I used to be an altar boy, one of those kids sweating uncomfortably in their black-and-white polyester robes. That was back before I realized that it was mostly made up.

Henry never told us how he got up to that bottom step, and it's been bugging me. All I can figure out is that he brought a ladder, or somehow swung a rope up. But where did the rope or ladder go? Maybe it's some sort of religious miracle—but I don't believe in miracles.

Take, for instance, the miracle that Father Haynes is about to perform.

The so-called miracle of Holy Communion is my least favorite part of the mass. It's the part where everybody gets up and stands in line to eat a communion wafer—what they call the host. Have you ever eaten a host?

I once read a short story about some cannibals who didn't turn their victims into steaks and chops and roasts; they made them all into sausages. Because when you're eating a sausage you don't think so much about what you're eating. It's the same with communion wafers.

Hosts are little white disks that do not resemble any kind of real food. The closest thing I can think of would be a flattened, sugarless marshmallow. They have almost no taste, just a faint sourness, and they require no chewing. I think they're made out of some kind of digestible paper.

My point is, the miracle of Holy Communion is when the priest turns these little white disks into the flesh of Jesus Christ. They call it transsubstantiation. So, if you buy that, then the host the priest places on your tongue is actually a sliver of Jesus meat. But they make the host as different from meat as they can, so that even though communion is a form of cannibalism, nobody gets grossed out. Like with the sausages.

Anyway, the reason I hate communion isn't the meat-eating component. I get hungry enough, I'll eat anything. The reason I hate it is because everybody in the church except me, Jason Bock, stands up and gets in line for their little snack. I sit there alone in the pew while everybody stares at me as they file past. I sit there and burn under the hellfire and damnation stare my father gives me. And I feel awful. But what choice do I have? According to Father Haynes, if a nonbeliever takes Holy Communion, he'll be damned for all eternity. Of course, being a nonbeliever damns me anyway, so I suppose it doesn't really matter, but I figure it's safer not to partake. Just in case I'm wrong about the whole God thing.

So I sit and endure the stares and the pangs and twinges of Catholic guilt, knowing that I am doing the right thing if I'm right, and the right thing even if I'm wrong.

Being Catholic is hard. Being ex-Catholic is even harder.

BUT A TIME CAME WHEN EVEN THE PLENITUDE OF LIFE FAILED TO SATISFY, AND SO THE OCEAN INSTILLED INTELLIGENCE AND FREE WILL IN CERTAIN OF ITS CREATURES, AND IT CALLED THEM HUMANS, AND IT WATCHED AS THE FIRST CRUDE TOOLS WERE FASHIONED BY HUMAN HANDS, AND IT WATCHED THE FIRST WARS BEING FOUGHT, AND IT WATCHED AS THESE LARGE-HEADED APES BEGAN TO RESHAPE THE LANDS AND THE WATERS IN NEW WAYS.

7

In the CTG, Tuesday is the Sabbath. Why, you ask? Because nothing else ever happens on a Tuesday. Shin, Dan, and I honor the Sabbath at Wigglesworth's, where we all order Magnum Brainblasters. Never had a Brainblaster? You should try one. It's a Wigglesworth specialty.

A Magnum Brainblaster is about a foot tall, green, foamy, and numbingly cold. For maximum impact, you drink it through a straw. Wigglesworth keeps his ingredients secret, but a Brainblaster certainly contains massive amounts of sugar, enough caffeine to wake up a corpse, and I think he throws in a chunk of dry ice just before serving. Think of it as Mountain Dew on steroids.

So we're sitting in the window table at Wigglesworth's Juiceteria, charging up on Brainblasters, and Shin, First Keeper of the Sacred Text, is showing us the Secret Dimensions he has calculated using Trigonometry, Guesswork, and other Holy Mathematical Techniques.

Overall height: 207 feet
Distance from ground to bottom of tank: 154 feet
Circumference of central column: 22 feet, 3 inches
Diameter of tank: 67 feet
Volume of tank: 1 million gallons
Weight of water: 8 million pounds
Distance between legs: 24 feet

. . . and so on. After Shin completes his presentation we stand up and bow in the direction of the Ten-legged God. Magda Price, who works for Wigglesworth part time, wanders over. She is wearing the official Wigglesworth Juiceteria uniform: a tight pink T-shirt with *Juicy!* printed across the front in lime-green script. On her it looks good.

"What are you guys doing?" she asks. Magda can't stand to be left out of anything.

"Honoring the Sabbath," I tell her.

"It's Tuesday."

"We are aware of that."

Magda wrinkles her forehead. For some reason it makes her look extra sexy. Not that she needs it. "The Sabbath is Sunday," she says.

"Not if you're Jewish."

"You're not Jewish. Besides, if you're Jewish the Sabbath is Saturday, and today is Tuesday."

"We are aware of that."

"Then you *know* it's not the Sabbath," she says, as if she's proved her point.

"We are Chutengodians," I say, making up the name on the spot. "Chutengodians celebrate the Sabbath on Tuesday."

"Chattenoogians?"

"Chutengodians. It's a religion."

"Oh. Is that what you were talking about the other day? At TPO? The ten leggy thing?"

"Ten *legged*," I say.

"It sounds like something you just made up."

"Blasphemy!"

"So what kind of religion is it?"

"The one true faith."

"Is it, like, a cult?"

"Not exactly."

Have you noticed that Magda and I are doing all the talking? Dan just stares at her like a lovesick dolphin, while Shin is paralyzed, in a world of his own. Dan is afraid to open his mouth because he knows he'll say something stupid, and Shin—well, Shin is so terrified of girls he's probably just hoping he won't crap in his pants. That's why what happens next is so bizarre.

"What do you worship?" Magda asks.

"The Ten-legged One," says Shin in a voice deeper than I've ever heard from him.

We all look at him, startled. He is staring at Magda with the sort of intensity he usually reserves for gastropods.

Magda says, "Is it some sort of giant spider?"

"Do not mock that which you do not understand," says Shin, still with the deep voice.

Dan catches my eye; I shrug. I quit trying to explain Shin years ago.

"I'm not mocking," says Magda.

"Well for you then that you are not," Shin intones. "For he is a jealous and vindictive god."

"Oh." Magda is giving Shin a cautious look. We all are. "What does he look like?"

"He is a god of many legs."

"Ten?"

"Precisely. He is a Great and Powerful God."

"How come I've never seen him?"

"But you have," says Shin.

I am wondering, who *is* this guy? He must be channeling a character from some video game. Probably seeing Magda Price as a collection of pixels. We all have our coping strategies.

Shin says, "You see him every day. In fact, you may look upon his holy visage now, if you dare." He points out the window at the silver dome of the tower rising above the buildings and trees.

Magda dares to look.

Shin says, "He is silver, he is proud, he glitters in the sun . . ."

"Omigod, are you talking about the *water tower*?"

"The Ten-legged One," Shin says, correcting her.

"You guys are worshipping a *water tower*?"

I decide to step in. "Think about it, Magda. What is the source of all life on Earth? Water. And where does water—"

I am just getting started when Magda interrupts me. "Can I join?"

"I thought you were a good little Catholic girl."

"Can't I be Catholic and Chutengodian at the same time?"

Like I said, Magda can't stand to be left out of anything.

Shin looks doubtful. "I'm not sure that females are permitted."

I frown and stroke my chin for effect. "I see no reason why the CTG should not admit one such creature. However, she is a rather small specimen." I look at Dan. "What do you think, First Acolyte Exaltus?"

Dan says, "We wouldn't want to be accused of sexual discrimination."

"True," I say. "Also, we may require breeding stock."

Magda's eyes grow wide. She grabs my Brainblaster and dumps it in my lap. I jump up with a howl, brushing crushed ice from my sodden crotch.

"Are you crazy?" I yell.

Dan is doubled over, laughing hysterically. I am dripping green juice all over the floor. Magda is standing with her arms crossed, her pretty lips tightened into a defiant smirk.

"The wench has spirit," says Shin.

THE OCEAN WATCHED WITH BOTH PRIDE AND TREPIDATION AS THE HUMANS DAMMED STREAMS AND RIVERS, DUG CANALS, BUILT ARTIFICIAL LAKES, AND POURED CHEMICALS INTO THE CLOUDS TO FORCE THEM TO RAIN. THE OCEAN WATCHED AS MOUNTAINS WERE LEVELED, AND SHAFTS WERE SUNK DEEP INTO THE EARTH, AND THE LIQUEFIED REMAINS OF ANCIENT FLORA AND FAUNA WERE SUCKED FROM DEEP IN THE CRUST AND MADE TO POWER GREAT MACHINES.

8

Apparently, it is possible to absorb Brainblaster directly through the skin, because by the time I get home with my sodden pants my mind is churning like a jet turbine. I've got a skull full of ideas—so many ideas I don't know which one to act on first. Here's a partial list.

1. Start work on CTG organizational chart.
2. List commandments.
3. Figure out who Shin was channeling.
4. The High Priestess: Am I too big and fat for her?
5. Figure out how Henry climbed the tower.
6. CTG holy days: note on calendar.
7. Climb tower.

And that's just the beginning. With Magda Price as our High Priestess—she insisted on the title—we now have a total of four members. The CTG is growing by leaps and bounds. By summer's end we might convert half of St. Andrew Valley. I could be like the guy that started the Mormon religion, or Scientology.

As I walk into the house, my mother pops her head around the corner.

"Where have you . . . what on earth happened to your pants?" she asks.

I *could* tell her that she is talking to the future religious leader of St. Andrew, but it's not the right moment.

"I spilled a drink on myself," I say.

"Well change into something nice . . . and dry, would you please? We have to leave in fifteen minutes."

"Leave for where?"

"What on earth is wrong with you, Jason? Don't you have a brain in your head? Are you feeling all right?"

"I'm fine. Where are we going?"

"I'm sure I told you. We're invited to dinner at your uncle Jack's."

"God, no."

"You keep a civil tongue in your head, young man. Now go get ready."

In the first place, Jack is not really my uncle, he's my dad's cousin. In the second place, he's a jerk. In the third place, he is the father of the insufferable Jack Bock Junior.

"Hey kid," Jack Bock Junior says to me. "How you doon?"

Jack Junior is wearing his golf clothes. At least I think they're golf clothes—yellow pants and a mint-green, short-sleeved shirt, tight across the chest. Where but on a golf course would you wear something like that? Jack Junior is a Serious Young Golfer.

"I'm 'doon' good, Jack."

"Attaboy," he says, clapping me on the shoulder. Jack is just one year older than me, but he treats me like a kid. "Going out for football this fall? We could use a big guy like you. Get you in shape." He jabs a forefinger into my belly. "Take off some a that mozzarella." In addition to being a Serious Young Golfer, Jack is quarterback of the St. Andrew Valley Vikings.

"I don't think so, Jack."

"Suit yourself."

We stand there by the swimming pool in his backyard, staring past each other, both of us wishing we were elsewhere. My parents are on the patio swilling gin and tonics and admiring Jack Senior's new $3,000 stainless-steel barbecue. Mrs. Jack is fussing over a plate of hors d'oeuvres.

Jack Junior says, "I hear you've been going to the Teen Power meetings. Aren't they great?" Jack Junior is Very Religious. He was an altar boy, too. He liked it a lot more than I did.

I say, "You're kidding me, right?"

"You don't like the meetings?"

"I'm not much into church stuff these days, Jack Junior." He hates it when I call him Jack Junior, so of course I do. "The fact is, I think it's all a load of crap."

He gapes at me as if I've told him I was a slime creature from the sixth dimension.

"What, are you—an *atheist*?"

"I'm a Chutengodian," I say.

"A . . . a what?" he asks, curiosity overcoming the fear and loathing.

"It's a cult."

He backs away from me a step. That gives me an idea.

"What sort of cult?"

I step toward him. "The Church of the Ten-legged God," I say with the widest, craziest smile I can muster. Jack Junior takes another step back. The swimming pool, filled with the lifeblood of the Ten-legged One, is only a few feet behind him. "It's the One True Faith, Jack. We do it all—sacrifice small animals, drink blood, worship Satan, the whole enchilada. You should come to one of our meetings."

"I don't *think* so." He tries to laugh it off, but I can see that part of him actually believes me.

"Join me in prayer, Jack Junior." I step toward him and thrust out my hands. "Take my hands. Pray with me. Pray to the Ten-legged One."

Horrified by my cultish fervor, Jack takes another step back and, with a huge splash, falls into the Ten-legged One's watery embrace.

✳   ✳   ✳

"I didn't push him."

"Well it certainly *looked* like you pushed him," my mother says.

"We were just talking."

"I've never been so embarrassed in my life."

"Maggie, if the boy says he didn't push him, he didn't push him."

"Thanks, Dad."

"You keep your mouth shut."

"That poor boy." My mother shaking her head. "He looked so miserable with his nice clothes all soaking wet."

"You could see right through his yellow pants."

"I told you to keep your mouth shut," my father snaps. For a few seconds we ride in silence, me in the backseat, my father driving, my mother clutching her purse. Then my father starts chuckling.

My mother looks at him. "What is it, dear?"

"I was just thinking," he says. "Whatever possessed that kid to wear purple briefs under those yellow pants?" He laughed again, and this time I joined him. Even my mother could not stop herself from shaking her head and smiling.

AND IT CAME TO PASS THAT THE LANDS AND THE WATERS BECAME STAINED WITH HUMAN FILTH, AND THE OCEAN BECAME CONCERNED.

9

The next morning, after my French toast and sausage and corn flakes and Pop Tart and orange juice and banana, (hey, a guy has to *eat*) I head straight over to the water tower and stare at the spiral staircase and try to figure out how Henry managed to get up there. It's been driving me nuts. All I can figure out is he had to have had help. Maybe he and his three stooges carried a ladder to the tower, Henry climbed up, then the stooges carried the ladder away. But why would they do that?

Besides, the one thing Henry *did* tell me was that he'd gotten up on his own. I believed him. Henry Stagg is a violent, psychotic fiend, but he's not a liar.

I am standing staring at the impossible-to-get-to spiral staircase when Shin shows up. He is surprised to see me.

"What are you doing here?" he asks.

"Trying to figure out how Henry got up there."

"How come you didn't call me?"

I shrug. It actually hadn't occurred to me. "What about you?"

Shin displays his notebook. "I'm working on something."

"Something gastropod?"

He shakes his head. "You'll see."

"Oh. Hey, the other day at Wigglesworth's. What was that about?"

"What do you mean?"

"You were acting sort of . . . different. When you were talking to Magda?"

"Oh. That wasn't me."

"Who was it?"

"I was channeling the Ten-legged One."

"Oh." I laugh. At least, I *think* he's making a joke. "Maybe we should change your title to First Speaker."

"Was it scary?"

"It didn't seem to scare the High Priestess."

"I don't think *she's* scared of *anything*."

I look up at the tower. "You think she'd be scared to climb the tower?"

"Who knows?"

We stand with our heads tipped back, looking up.

Shin says, "Have you figured it out?"

I glare at the spiral stairway and shake my head. "He says he flew. Maybe he did."

*　　*　　*

The small, boxy houses on Ensign Avenue all look exactly the same. Except for the address numbers. The number I'm looking for is 1803.

There are a lot of streets with small, boxy, identical houses in St. Andrew Valley. According to my dad, they were all built just after World War II, cheap and fast, because the soldiers coming home needed places to live. I suppose most of the original owners are dead by now, or really old. Anyway, that was a long time ago.

Number 1803 is at the end of the block. I press the doorbell and wait. A few seconds later Henry Stagg opens the door. He is wearing nothing but a pair of black boxer shorts.

"Hey, is that Jay-boy?"

"Hi, Henry."

"What's going on?" He peers past me. "Where's your shadow?"

"You mean Shin?"

"Schinner, yeah."

"He's busy."

"Oh. You want to come in?"

"Sure." I follow him into the house. As soon as I enter I know why he's walking around in his under-wear—the house has no air-conditioning. "You the only one here?"

"My sister and my folks are all at work." He opens the refrigerator. "You want a Coke or something?"

This is the friendliest I've ever seen Henry. He seems almost normal.

"Coke would be great."

He hands me a cold can and we pop them open.

"So what's up?" he asks.

"Not much. What about you?"

"I was just sitting around reading."

"*You?*"

He looks hurt. "What, you don't think I can read?"

"You just don't seem the bookish type. What are you reading?"

"*Lord of the Rings.* Again."

"You ever read any of his other books?"

"Just *The Hobbit.* I don't read much fantasy. I like sci-fi better."

I listen to him name his favorites—Larry Niven, Vernor Vinge, Robert Heinlein—and am more amazed with each writer he names. Do I know this guy? What ever happened to Henry Stagg, the illiterate psychotic fiend?

We go to his room, which is very neat and organized— another surprise. He shows me his collection of sci-fi novels. He must have a couple hundred of them, all arranged in alphabetical order in a big metal bookshelf. Turns out we've read a lot of the same books and I realize, jealously, that Henry Stagg has read more books than I have. Unless you count comic books.

We sit on the floor in front of his oscillating fan and talk sci-fi, and I am thinking how strange this is that I should be sitting peacefully with Henry Stagg in his bedroom when only a week or so ago he punched me in the face for no reason whatsoever. I don't even mind how hot it is. The psycho-barbarian turns out to have a brain after all.

Eventually, I get around to the reason I came by.

"Tell me something," I say. "Seriously. How did you get up on the water tower?"

"I told you."

"I mean really."

Henry gives me a measuring look. "Why do you want to know?"

"I want to go up."

"And get caught by Kramer?"

"I'd go up at night."

"Okay, suppose I take you up. Are you going to tell me what you and Schinner and Danny are up to?"

"Up to?"

"Yeah. I know you guys are cooking up something."

I think about it for a few seconds, then decide to just go for it.

"We started a new religion."

Henry is waiting for more. I guess I have to give it to him.

"We worship the water tower."

He is nodding now, his face eager.

"We're Chutengodians," I say.

"Yeah? Who's we?"

"Me and Shin and Dan. And Magda."

His eyebrows pop up. "Magda Price?"

"Yeah."

"Okay then," he says.

"Okay what?"

"Okay, then I wanna be a Chutengodian too."

A ND SO THE OCEAN SENT A MESSAGE TO THE HUMAN LEADERS AND DID THEREBY CAUSE THEM TO ERECT THOUSANDS OF GREAT EFFIGIES OF ITSELF THROUGHOUT THE LAND. AND IN EACH OF THESE TOWERS THE OCEAN DEPOSITED A TINY PORTION OF ITS PURE SELF, AND GAVE THE HUMANS PERMISSION TO PARTAKE OF IT FREELY. AND THE HUMANS GATHERED AROUND THE TOWERS AND BUILT THEIR TOWNS AND CITIES AROUND THEM, AND THE TOWERS DID SERVE AS THE EYES AND EARS OF THE OCEAN, AND THE OCEAN WATCHED AND LISTENED AND WAITED, AND FOR A TIME, THE OCEAN WAS CONTENT.

10

At precisely fifteen minutes after midnight, I slip out of bed and look out my window to the east. Just past the corner of the garage, through the branches of the elm tree, I can see the blinking red light on top of the water tower. The Ten-legged One beckons me. I quietly dress in ninja black, right down to my Reeboks, and silently slink down the hall, slither past my parents' bedroom, and ooze out the back door.

Free, free at last! Ha! They'll never catch me now—not until it's too late. Too late for everyone! They'll regret their laughter and taunts. They'll regret throwing me in their reeking dungeons. I've eaten my last plague-ridden rat. I'll mount the Ten-legged One and gallop from the river to the sea, crushing all who stand in my way. Nyuh-ha-ha! From now on, *they'll* do as *I* say.

It takes me twenty minutes to reach the tower. No Henry. I sit with my back against one of the legs and wait, listening to the soft sound of water droplets hitting grass, thinking deep thoughts about Chutengodianism. What's it like in Chutengodian heaven? *Is* there a Chutengodian heaven? And if there's a heaven, does that mean there's a hell? Serious questions requiring serious thought.

I hear a soft sound; cowboy boots scuffing grass. Henry appears on the opposite side of the tower, hands stuffed in his pockets, pacing. He doesn't see me. I watch him for a few seconds. I'm about to let him know I'm there when he steps behind the tower leg. I wait for him to come out the other side.

Thirty seconds later I'm still waiting.

"Henry!" I say. No response. I walk over to where I saw him. No Henry. I raise my voice. "Hey, Henry!"

"Right here." The voice comes from above—I about jump out of my skin.

"Henry?" I look up and see him thirty feet above me, clinging to the leg.

"Come on," he says. "Grab onto the cables."

"Cables?" I see them now, four thick black cables running up the channel of the I-beam. "What are they?"

"I dunno. Electric cables, I guess. You coming or not?"

Henry continues his climb, wedging the toes of his cowboy boots between the cables and pulling himself up,
hand over hand.

If I think too long about this I won't do it. I grab a
cable and pull myself up. It's surprisingly easy, easier
than the rope climb in gym class. The cables are covered
with grippy black plastic, and my toes wedge nicely
between them. I get into a rhythm: left hand, right foot,
right hand, left foot.

"How you doing?" Henry says over his shoulder.

"I'm okay." The catwalk is still a long way above us.

"Don't look down."

Of course I look down. We can't be more than fifty or
sixty feet up, but it looks like a mile. My heart thumps
wildly and a prickly feeling runs up my back.

"I told you not to look," Henry says.

I wrench my eyes away from the ground and wait for
my heartbeat to slow. My hands are locked on the
cables, and my knees are shaking.

"You okay?" Henry asks.

"No."

"We're almost there."

I look up. Henry is still about twenty feet above me.

"Just keep climbing," he says.

I slide my right hand up a couple feet and grab the
cable. I move my left foot up, jam it between the cables,
and move up another foot.

"You got it," he says, and starts climbing again. The
catwalk seems an impossible distance above him, but he

is soon closer to the tank than he is to me.

"Forget it," I say to myself. "This is nuts."

I watch Henry swing himself onto the catwalk. His face is a small moon against the planetary mass of the tank.

"You comin'?"

"No."

"C'mon. It's not that hard."

"I'm going back down."

"You're already halfway."

"I could get killed. This is crazy!"

"Crazy? Man, you want to see crazy?" With a maniacal laugh, Henry drops over the edge of the catwalk and hangs by his hands. *This* is *crazy.*"

"Don't *do* that."

"You better get up here. Help, I'm gonna fall!"

"Cut it out, Henry."

He lets go with one hand. "Look at me, I'm a monkey."

"Henry, please . . ."

He grabs the edge and swings himself back up onto the catwalk, laughing. My fear gives way to anger. "That was really stupid, man."

"Me stupid? Look at you. Halfway up and stuck like a cat in a tree."

"I'm not stuck." To prove it, I move my right hand and slide my right foot down a few inches. I can get back down if I want to. But just moving that little bit—plus being really pissed at Henry—is enough to restore my confidence. If Henry can do it, so can I. Once again I begin to climb. Left hand, right foot, right hand, left foot. My arms are aching and my calves are cramping. Left hand, right foot, right hand . . . after an eternity I reach the catwalk and flop down on my back on the steel grating, gasping for breath. A hundred twenty feet? No problem. I could've climbed 121.

"Didn't think you had it in you, Jay-boy," Henry says.

"Don't worry, I got it in me." I sit up, gripping the safety rail with both hands.

"Wait till you get up top. C'mon." Henry walks casually to the end of the catwalk and climbs up the ladder to the higher catwalk, the one that wraps all the way around the tank. I'm feeling pretty rubbery in the legs, but compared to scaling that leg, the ladder looks like a piece of cake.

As long as I don't look down.

I am sitting at the exact center of the top of the tank, where the steps end. The tank slopes rapidly away on every side—there is no flat area. Imagine standing on an enormous metal ball—that's what it's like. I can't see any of the I-beams or girders or any of the superstructure. I might as well be on a small metal moon hanging high above the surface of the Earth.

Beneath me is a hatch about two feet across, secured by a brass padlock. Next to that is a four-foot-high steel post holding up a blinking red warning light. I have my arms wrapped around the post, afraid to let go. Every three seconds the top of the tower is lit up by a red flash.

Looking at the tank's horizon makes my stomach spin; I raise my eyes to the real horizon. I can see for miles. I see tens of thousands of flickering lights—neon signs, streetlamps, lights in windows. I see the moving lights of cars and trucks, and the garish, stabbing lights from the casino outside of town, and beyond that a glow on the horizon: the lights of Fairview, more than twenty miles away.

"I love it up here," Henry says. He is lying on his back, spread-eagled on the sloping steel, his head six feet from the hatch. Another few feet and he'd slide right off into space.

"Why do you suppose they have this hatch padlocked?" I ask. "They afraid somebody's gonna steal the water?"

"I think they're more worried about terrorists."

"Yeah, right. Terrorists in St. Andrew Valley."

"You never know," Henry says. "Hey, you know what would be funny? Get a few gallons of red food coloring and dump it in the water. Everybody would turn on their faucets and it'd be like blood coming out."

"You'd need a lot of food coloring. There's a million gallons of water in there."

"Or you could dump soap in it."

"Why would you do that?"

"I don't know. It'd be funny. People foaming at the mouth."

"You've got a weird sense of humor, Henry."

"I've heard that."

After a few minutes I start to relax. I loosen my death grip on the post and stand up. My stomach is floating and I have an empty spot under my heart. That means I'm afraid. But I also have a turbine whining in my skull, and a shuddery feeling high in my chest—feelings of power and excitement.

"I feel like Moses," I say. "Moses on the mountain. You know what we need? Some commandments."

"I got enough trouble dealing with the first ten," Henry says.

"Ours will be easier. Like, 'Thou shalt not pollute the water supply,' or, 'Thou shalt not eat asparagus.'"

"You don't like asparagus?"

"Not much."

"I don't mind it. I like how it makes my pee smell. Hey, if the water tower is god, what's the devil?"

"I don't think the Chutengodians have a devil."

"You gotta have a devil. You can't have a religion without a devil."

"Sure you can. Buddhists don't have a devil."

"I still think you need a devil. Hey, y'know what'd be cool? Come up here in a thunderstorm."

"You'd get fried," I say.

"You think so?"

"This is the tallest structure in St. Andrew Valley. I bet it gets hit by lightning all the time."

"Oh. Well, it would be fun while it lasted."

"Hey, you know what we should do?" I say. "Get everybody up here. All the Chutengodians. In fact, we gotta do it. Next Tuesday, the Sabbath, we all climb up for Midnight Mass."

Henry tips his head back and looks at me. "This is my territory."

"It would just be for an hour or so. Tell you what. You can be the High Priest."

Henry thinks about that.

"What does the High Priest have to do?"

ONE DAY THE OCEAN NOTICED THAT THE HUMANS WERE PASSING BY ITS EFFIGIES WITH HARDLY AN UPWARD GLANCE, AND DRINKING FREELY WITHOUT THANKS OR ACKNOWLEDGMENT.

11

"Jason! Jason, wake up!"

"I'm up. I'm awake. What's the matter?"

"Are you feeling all right?"

"I'm fine, Mom. Jeez." I pull the covers up over my head.

"It's almost eleven!" She tugs on the bedspread. "You can't sleep the whole day away."

"Why not?" Actually, I probably *could* sleep all day.

A few hours ago, Henry Stagg and I watched the sun rise over St. Andrew Valley from the top of the Ten-legged One. The town was still in shadow when the sun's first rays lit up our faces. We sat in devout silence as sunlight touched the silver tank, lighting it inch by inch, from the top down. Talk about being close to God.

"It's not natural to sleep fourteen hours a day."

I lower the covers and look up at her. "I haven't been sleeping that long. I was up most of the night."

"Aren't you feeling well?"

"I'm *fine*. I was having a religious experience."

She gives me her worried, disbelieving look—a look I know well. I swing my legs over the edge of the mattress and sit up.

"Okay, okay, I'm up already. You happy now?"

"I'd be happier if you weren't such a smart mouth." Now she gives me her pissed-off, you'll-pay-for-this-young-man look.

"Sorry," I say—and I really am. My mother can get very sulky when she doesn't get treated right. And sulky usually translates to innumerable demands for help with un-fun things like yard work, basement cleaning, and attendance at extra-boring church functions. I decide to head her off at the pass. I look out the window. "Looks like another hot day. Guess I better get busy."

"Oh? Doing what?"

"I want to get the lawn mowed before it gets too hot out."

She looks shocked, and why not? This will be the first time I've ever mowed the lawn without direct orders from a superior officer. Better to take on one quick job than let my mother enslave me for some major all-day monotony.

"If you'd gotten up like any normal person you'd be done with it by now," she says, but I see the sulk draining out of her, and I know I made the right move.

✳ ✳ ✳

The problem with little jobs is that they sometimes turn into big jobs. I have the lawn one-quarter mowed when the mower sputters and coughs and dies. Diagnosis? Fuel crisis. Need gasoline. Call Kuwait. Raid an oil tanker. Drill a well.

Or walk into the garage and grab the big red gas can off the shelf.

Unfortunately, the big red gas can is bone dry. I remember now. I used it up last time I mowed the stupid lawn. I stomp into the house, making plenty of noise.

"Mom!"

No answer.

"MOM!"

I hear a muffled response. I clomp up the stairs. "We're out of gas!"

"What's that, honey?" Her voice is coming from the bathroom.

"We're out of *gas*," I say to the bathroom door. "I need you to drive me to the gas station."

"Honey, I just got in the tub. You'll have to walk."

"Mom, it's like a *mile*."

"It won't hurt you to get a little exercise."

"I don't have any money."

"My purse is on the kitchen counter."

I take a breath and almost say something more . . . but then I don't. It wouldn't do any good. When my mother takes a bath in the middle of the day, it's serious business. She probably has bubbles up to her chin and a stack of magazines.

I grab a twenty out of her purse and the empty gas can out of the garage and slog off down Decatur to Cedar Lake Road, then left toward the Amoco station. Step, step, step, step—this is very boring. I am bored. I am walking with an empty red plastic container, with fifty miles of trackless desert waste between me and the Amoco oasis. If I keep walking I might make it by midday tomorrow. With each step the gas can hits my right knee. I switch hands, and now it brushes my left knee. Step, swishstep, step, swishstep. I try hanging the can over my shoulder, and for about fifty steps that feels okay, but then my elbow starts to hurt, and I switch shoulders. Only 49.95 miles to go. I try balancing the can on my head, but it presses the top button of my baseball cap into the center of my skull. I go back to Plan A: Step, swishstep, step, swishstep. . . .

Night comes and goes, I follow the ridge of a sand dune that stretches to the horizon, I fight off a pack of insane meercats, I struggle blindly through a sandstorm. Hours later, parched and choking on Saharan grit, I spy the waving fronds of a date palm beyond the next rocky ridge. A mirage? I stay the course—step, swishstep, step, swishstep—and drag myself to the shimmering edge of the oasis. There it is, the artesian well. I plug a handful of shekels into its gaping slot and, with my last iota of energy, I punch the Mountain Dew button.

Ka-chunk! Jackpot! The intrepid wanderer wins again. I pop the top and pour all twelve ounces down my throat.

"Ahhh," I say to no one in particular. I look out past the Amoco sign, past the utility lines and treetops to the rounded silver dome of the Ten-legged One. Watching me. I salute with my empty Mountain Dew can and say, "Thank you, oh Great and Powerful One."

"You talking to me?"

My heart thumps, then I realize it's just Milt, standing in the doorway of the repair bay smoking a cigarette.

"Hey, Milt."

"What happen, you run out of gas?"

"The lawn mower did."

Milt nods, flicks his cigarette toward the pumps, and goes back to work on somebody's minivan. I go to the pumps, stepping on his smoldering butt on the way, fill up my five-gallon can, pay for the gas, grab the can, and head for home.

I have walked only a few yards when I realize my mistake. Stubbornly, I keep walking. After a hundred steps I decide to try holding the can in front of my legs with both hands. Then I try propping it up on my shoulder. Then I set it down and try to compute how much five gallons of gasoline weighs.

Shin calculated that the Ten-legged One contains one million gallons of water that weighs eight million pounds. By employing my remarkable mathematical skills, I deduce that one gallon of H_2O weighs eight pounds. Gasoline must weigh pretty close to that, I figure. Brilliant!

So how come, knowing that I would have to transport it on foot across fifty miles of trackless desert waste, I went ahead and filled the gas can with forty pounds of liquid when I only need a half gallon or so to finish mowing the lawn? Idiocy!

I consider pouring some of the gas down the sewer, but the Ten-legged One would not approve. Gasoline is very bad for the water. I *could* haul the can back to the Amoco station, leave it in Milt's care, then go home empty-handed and beg my mother for a ride. Not a bad plan, but kinda embarrassing. Then I catch a brainwave. Shin lives just three blocks up Louisiana Avenue. Shin has a wagon, an old red metal job he's had ever since he was a little kid. Just what I need. An oil tanker. Amazing! Brilliant! The kid scores yet another cerebral coup. The intelligentsia are astonished by Jason Bock's remarkable powers of reasoning.

Bock! (they cry from the gallery, standing in their academic robes on their chairs stomping their feet and pumping their fists) *Bock! Bock! Bock!*

"It was nothing," I say, smiling at their childish display of admiration. "I merely examined every possibility and made a carefully considered judgment as to the best course of action."

Bock! Bock! Bock!

"Thank you," I say. "Thank you very much."

ND THE OCEAN WAS SAD, FOR IT HAD LAVISHED
MUCH LOVE ON THESE STRANGE, THIRSTY APES.
YET THEY GAVE NOT THE SLIGHTEST GESTURE OF
RESPECT TO THEIR MAKER, AND THEY TREATED THE
GREAT EFFIGIES AS THEY MIGHT TREAT A HOUSE OF
WOOD, OR A PILE OF STONE.

12

"Guess where I was at five o'clock this morning."

"Not in bed."

"How'd you know that?"

"If you were in bed you wouldn't have asked me where I thought you were." Shin carefully lifts his little red wagon from the hook on the garage wall. "You're going to be careful with it, aren't you?"

"As if it were my own. So, if I wasn't in bed, where was I?"

Shin scrunches up his mouth and bites his cheek, making him look like a guy trying to eat himself.

"You were having breakfast with Elvis Presley."

"That was last week."

"Then I give up." He rolls the wagon back and forth

on the garage floor. "You aren't going to ride it down any hills, are you?"

"I'm going to use it to transport one five-gallon can of unleaded. That's all. You want to know where I was or not?"

"Okay."

"I was standing on God's head."

Shin's jaw drops.

"I climbed the Ten-legged One," I say, just in case he didn't get it the first time.

Shin's eyes bulge.

I laugh at his goofy expression. "I climbed up with Henry."

Shin is hugging himself and his eyes are full and suddenly I understand that he isn't clowning, he's really upset.

"What's wrong?" I say.

"You went without me?"

"No! I mean, yes, but it wasn't like that. I just went to meet Henry there. He was gonna show me how he gets up there."

"Why didn't you *call* me?"

"I didn't . . . it wasn't . . ."

I am about to lie to my best friend. Because the real reason I didn't call him was because I knew Henry would act like a jerk around him, and Shin would do his whiny Shin thing, and Henry would laugh at us both and I would never find out how he climbed the water tower. I am going to lie to Shin because I could never tell him what a pathetic nerd he looks like to a guy like Henry Stagg. Even though he knows. But he will never hear it from me.

"He made me promise to come alone," I say.

Shin is shaking his head.

"I had to swear to go alone," I say, underscoring the lie. "I didn't know we were actually going to climb up."

Shin blinks and a tear dribbles down his cheek. I want to grab him and slap him and tell him, *Grow up. Don't be such a baby. If you weren't such a nerdy, clumsy wuss, you wouldn't get left out.* At the same time I feel awful for not telling him about Henry sooner. Shin is, after all, Keeper of the Sacred Text. And he's my friend. And he trusts me.

"Look," I say, "I'm sorry. I should have told you."

He nods, and I am afraid he understands completely, even the part I didn't say.

"Anyway, I know how we can get up there now."

"How?" he asks in a small voice.

"You climb up one of the legs."

"How?"

"There are some cables to grab onto. It's not that hard." As soon as I say that I regret it, because for Shin to climb up that leg . . . well, I can hardly imagine it. He's no Spider-Man.

Shin licks his lips. "I want to go up."

"Actually, it's not *that* easy."

"Tonight." He sets his jaw. "Take me up tonight."

Resistance is futile.

"Okay," I say. "Tonight. Wear black."

"What time?" Shin asks.

"I'll come by at midnight." I lift the gas can into the wagon. "I gotta go mow some grass." I grab the wagon handle and start down the driveway. I look back. Shin waves, smiling.

I decide to wait till later to tell him that Henry is our new High Priest.

By the time I finish mowing the lawn it is ninety degrees out and I'm sweating buckets. I drag myself into the house and down a carton of orange juice.

"Good lord, Jason," says my mother.

I set the empty carton down. "I was thirsty," I say.

"That was an entire half gallon of juice."

"It was half empty."

"Nevertheless! Are you feeling all right?"

"I'm just hot. It's hot out there."

"We should get you in for a blood test. Your granduncle Herman had diabetes, you know. It's in our family. How many times have you urinated today?"

"Mom! I'm not sick; I'm just hot and thirsty."

She shakes her head. "Well, let's keep an eye on you. Oh, by the way, one of your friends called."

"Who?"

"I'm sure I don't remember." She points at the notepad next to the phone. "I wrote her name and number."

Her? I grab the notepad. My mother's scrawl could be read in any number of ways—Mopdo, Waqude, AArgha—but I'm pretty sure the name she meant to write is Magda.

13

"I called to apologize," Magda says.

"Oh. For what?"

"For dumping that drink on you, silly."

"Oh."

"I feel bad about it. I knew you were just kidding around."

"Oh . . ." I sound like a moron. Is "Oh" all I know how to say? "Uh . . . that's okay." A moronic moron. Zog the Neanderthal. I'm sweating like a pig (do pigs really sweat?) and I can smell my armpits. Good thing there's five miles of phone line between us.

"You're not going to tell my boss about it, are you? I could get fired."

"Uh, no . . ."

"Not that working at Wigglesworth's is so great anyway."

"At least you got a job."

"Next time you come in and I'm working, I'll give you a free Brainblaster."

"You don't have to."

"I want to. So, how's it going?"

What does she mean by that? I don't know what to say. It's weird. I can sit in a TPO meeting or a classroom with a bunch of kids and yak my head off. Or talk for hours to Shin, or even to a guy like Henry, but one-on-one with Magda, my brain seizes up like an overheated engine.

"Jason? You there?"

"Yeah."

"You fall asleep or something?"

"No. My mom thinks I've got narcolepsy." *Why am I telling her this?*

"What's that?"

"Sleeping sickness." *Shut up, you idiot! Do you want her to think you've got some tropical disease?* "But I'm not sleepy right now."

"'Cause if you want to sleep we could talk later."

"I'm okay." I hope my sweat dripping into the little mouthpiece holes won't short out the phone.

"So, how's the new religion going?"

"Going? Uh . . . I climbed up the tower last night."

"You did? Really?"

"Yeah. Me and Henry went up."

"Henry *Stagg*?"

"Yeah."

"He's . . . I didn't know you guys were friends."

"We're not friends really. But he's okay."

"I think he's scary. I heard he hit you or something."

"Where'd you hear that?"

"Some kids were talking about it."

Great. All of St. Andrew Valley is talking about how little Henry Stagg laid me out with a single punch.

"So did he?" Magda is nothing if not persistent.

"Yeah, but that was last week. He's a Chutengodian now. Chutengodians don't hit each other."

"So what was it like?"

"To get hit?"

"No! To climb up the tower."

"It was cool. You can see all the way to Fairview."

"I think I'd be scared. I mean, I'd *do* it, but I'd be scared."

I don't know what she means by that. Does she mean she wants to climb the tower?

"Jason?"

"What?"

"So are you mad at me?"

"Why would I be mad at you?"

"I don't know. You aren't saying anything."

"Oh." I'm glad *I'm* not trying to have a conversation with me. It must be boring as hell. What can I say that is interesting? Perhaps an astute grammatical observation.

I say, "Did you know that you start a lot of sentences with the word *so*?"

"Thanks a lot. Did you know you're an insensitive jerk?"

Hmmm. Maybe she's not into grammar.

"Sorry," I say. "I just thought you might want to know."

"Yeah, well, thanks a lot. Like I need language lessons from a guy who can't have a simple phone conversation."

"I didn't mean anything by it."

Silence.

I say, "Look, lots of people say stuff like that. Like 'y'know.' Some people say 'y'know' about ten times a minute. Y'know what else? A lot of people say *actually* all the time. I do it myself."

"I've noticed."

"Really?"

"*Actually,* I've got better things to do than pick on how my friends talk. *So* . . . will you take me up next time?"

"You *actually* want to climb the water tower?"

"*So* . . . isn't that what Chatenoogians do?"

"Not Chate*noo*gians. Chuten*god*ians. You *actually* want to go up there?"

"*Actually,* I do."

At precisely midnight, the uber-ninja emerges from the darkness. He stands at the edge of the smudge of light cast by Professor Peter Schinner's office window. Inside, Professor Schinner is hunched over his thesis. He is hard at work, a labor that will prove lethal for the young professor, for the thesis contains the ancient secrets stolen from the ninja, secrets that must never see the light of day.

Still, the uber-ninja hesitates, fingering the razor-sharp points of a *shuriken,* for Professor Schinner is in fact his brother, captured at birth by missionaries, trained from an early age in the esoteric arts of detection by a cabal of insane Franciscan monks.

The ninja knows that Schinner must die, but to kill him he must also destroy himself. Two brothers, both brilliant, both the best of the best, doomed to mutual self-destruction . . .

I rap on the glass. Shin's head jerks up. He squints at me through the window, looks at the clock, then motions me around to the side door.

"You planning to climb the tower in your X-men pajamas?" I ask when he opens the door.

"Shhh! I had to put 'em on for my mom. She always comes down to say good night. Give me a couple minutes."

I follow him to his room. He strips out of his pajamas. I can't believe how skinny the guy is. You can count his ribs. He digs around in a pile of dirty clothes.

"Wear something dark," I tell him.

"I know, I know."

While he dresses, I sit at his desk and look at the sketchbook he was working on. The open page is covered with Shin's tight, crabbed printing. Shin used to cover the pages of his sketchbooks with ornate drawings of buildings and machines, but lately he's been writing more and drawing less.

"What are you working on?" I ask. "Some snail notes?"

"Not exactly."

I start reading:

. . . and lo! The Ocean spake, and his words did cause Men and Women to quail and cry out in fear for themselves and their children and even for their children's children's children and beyond, for though the planet might spin through space for all Eternity, it was suddenly made known to all that Mankind's grip upon this planet of fire and ice was but a momentary scrabbling across its slippery surfaces, for lo! The Ocean did speak the words of Truth and Justice and the Watery Way upon which all must eventually drown or be crushed by the pounding waves of anger and rage and fury and hatred, and lo! It was revealed upon this Holy Day of Holy Days that the evil Men do must ever be visited back upon them with vengeance and justice and bloodshed, for the blood shall flow with the Water of Life, even as Life departs.

I look up. Shin, watching me, puts on a pair of jeans and a purple T-shirt.

"What is this?" I ask.

"Genesis," Shin says.

"Genesis?"

"The first Book of the Sacred Text," he says. "I'm the First Keeper, right?"

"Yeah, but . . . *wow.*" I read a little more.

And so spake the Ocean, and the seas and lakes
and rivers and puddles did carry His Words. And
every drop of rain and every snowflake and every
bead of sweat did carry His Words. And every driblet
of snot and piss and vomit did carry His Words.

And His Words swam across the earth in a great
flood of sacred knowledge, and lo! The Ocean was not
yet satisfied that all had heard, and so he caused
his body to swell and rise and sweep over the deltas,
the lowlands, the plains, the mesas, the mountains. . . .

"This is some wild stuff. Where'd you get it?"

"It just sort of comes out. I started writing it last week."

I flip back through the notebook. There are about
sixty pages covered with Shin's minute script, with a few
tiny drawings of water towers mixed in. Some of the
water towers are airborne, jetting across the page.

"You wrote all this in a week?" I read the first lines
from the first page:

In the beginning was the Ocean. And the Ocean was alone.

"I don't get it. What ocean?"

"All of them. They're all connected, you know."

And the Ocean did not know where it ended or
where it began, and so it created Time. And the
Ocean passed through Time.

* * *

I flip through the notebook. Page after page after page.

Shin says, "It's like it's not even me writing. I just watch the pen move across the page. I think maybe I'm channeling him."

"Channeling who?"

"The Ten-legged One."

We lock eyes for a few seconds and I swear to god— whatever god you want—I have absolutely no idea whether or not he's kidding.

AT FIRST, THE HUMANS DID NOT UNDERSTAND WHAT THE OCEAN WAS SAYING. THEY HEARD ONLY CREAKS AND GROANS AND THE WHISTLING OF THE WIND. BUT ONE HUMAN, GREAT OF INTELLIGENCE AND GREAT OF SENSITIVITY, HEARD THE OCEAN'S WORDS, AND LO! HE BEGAN TO SPEAK WITH THE OCEAN'S VOICE.

14

Being the leader of a growing religion is not all power and glory. For one thing, there is way too much politics. In other words, you have to lie a lot.

On this day, the Founder and Head Kahuna of the Chutengodians uttered four lies.

First, I told Magda that I would take her up the next time I climbed the water tower. But I knew that I would be going up with Shin that very night, so I couldn't invite her to come. Why? Because I was sure that Shin would fail. There was no way a skinny, bookish, snail-raising guy like Shin could monkey his way up that leg, and I didn't want him to fail in front of Magda. That was a good lie, I told myself.

Second, I did not tell Shin that I made Henry Stagg the new High Priest of the CTG. Sooner or later Shin will find out. He'll probably sulk for days. Shin is a delicate fellow. I don't like to see him upset.

Third, I did not tell Shin that I didn't believe he could actually climb the tower leg.

Fourth, as Shin was struggling to climb the first twenty feet up the tower leg, I shouted down to him, "C'mon Shin, you can do it!" even though I knew he could not.

I never used to lie to my friends this way, especially Shin. And now here I am, thirty feet up God's leg, while a few feet below me the First Keeper of the Sacred Text is frozen in place, too terrified to move.

"It's okay," I say—another lie. It's not okay. "Just relax, then move one foot down a few inches."

"My legs won't move."

"Yes they will."

"Help me."

"I can't climb over you, Shin."

Shin does not reply.

"You're only twenty feet from the ground. Even if you fall you'll probably survive."

Maybe that was the wrong thing to say.

"Shin?"

Uh-oh. I look down. Shin is clinging to the leg, not moving at all. He's gone into his shell. Now what? I can't climb over him or around him so, as the saying goes, there's no place to go but up. So up I go.

It's easier this time, because I know I can do it. Also, I'm worried about Shin. I don't know how long he can hang on. Maybe seconds; maybe hours. I reach the catwalk, head straight across to the spiral staircase, and climb down. At the bottom of the staircase I let myself hang by my hands—I hate this part—and let go. I hit feet first and roll like a paratrooper, then run over to Shin. He's still hanging on.

"Shin? You okay up there?"

Nothing. I grab the cables and climb up to a point just below his feet.

"Shin? I'm right here." I touch one of his ankles. "Right below you."

He makes a sound, something like "Urgh." I take that as a good sign.

"I'm gonna grab your foot and move it, okay?" Without waiting for another "urgh," I clasp his right foot in my hand and slowly pull it out from where he has it wedged between the cables, move it down six inches, and shove it back. He doesn't resist, but he isn't exactly helping.

"I'm right here. I'm not going to let you fall." Another lie? I hope not. "You gotta move one of your hands now, Shin. Do it slow, like a snail. I won't let you fall."

"Okay," he says in a small voice.

I wait. It takes almost a minute, but finally he manages to loosen his death grip on the cable and slide it down.

"Okay, now your other foot." I tap his ankle to let him know which one. A few seconds later he twists his foot and wriggles it out from between the cables and moves it down. "You got it, buddy, I say. Now your other hand . . ."

Five minutes later we are down. Shin is squatting on the ground, his arms wrapped around his knees, shaking.

"I'm useless," he says.

"No you're not."

"I froze up."

"Look, Spidey, it ain't that easy. I froze up too."

"You did?"

"Henry had to talk me up."

"What did he do—threaten to slime you?"

"No. . . . Would that have worked on you?"

"I don't even remember. We were climbing, and it was really hard. My arms hurt and I was starting to get dizzy . . . then all of a sudden you were underneath me, talking." He gives me a startled look. "How did you get underneath me?"

"I took a shortcut," I say, pointing up.

Shin is rocking back and forth. "Some First Keeper I am. The Ten-legged One won't even let me climb him."

He looks so miserable that I say, "Sure he will. The Ten-legged One was just testing you. I know a way to get you up there. I mean, you're coming to Midnight Mass, right?"

"Midnight Mass?"

"Next Tuesday."

"This is the first I've heard about it."

"I just decided. The entire CTG is going up. All of us."

"Even Magda?"

"Sure. Why not?"

He tips his head back and stares up at the belly of the

god. "You really think you can get me up there?"

"Absolutely," I say with complete confidence. "I have a plan."

But, of course, I'm lying again.

The next day I happen to decide to take a walk, and I happen to walk in a southeasterly direction, and I happen to be walking past Wigglesworth's Juiceteria when I happen to glance through the front window and happen to notice the Chutengodian High Priestess behind the juice bar blending a raspberry smoothie. I happen to open the door and walk inside.

"Hey," I say, suave as can be.

"Hi, Jason," Magda says, smiling.

"I came to collect my free Brainblaster."

"Coming right up." She grabs a clean blender bowl and starts adding ingredients.

"What's in those things, anyway?"

"It's a secret."

"There are no secrets between Chutengodians."

"If I tell you, I could get fired."

"Just tell me what makes 'em green. It's not asparagus, is it?"

Magda leans across the counter and whispers, "Kiwi fruit."

"Ah!" I watch as she blends the kiwi concoction into a wicked-looking froth.

"There you go." She hands me the cup, then says with a grin, "Don't spill it this time."

"I'll try not to." I take a sip. "Well blended!"

"I'm a professional." She is looking right at me and smiling. I feel all foamy inside, and I don't think it's the Brainblaster.

"You still want to climb the tower?" I ask.

She nods, making her eyes big.

"We're thinking Tuesday night."

"Will Henry be there?"

"Um . . . I think so."

"Good, that sounds like fun."

"Good? I thought you didn't like Henry."

"I just think he's kind of scary."

"Oh."

"But *interesting.*"

I slurp my Brainblaster. Uh-oh. Too much. The pain hits me high on my forehead. I squeeze my eyes shut. *Ow, ow, ow!*

"You okay?"

"Brain freeze," I gasp, my eyes watering.

I hear Magda's laugh and the pain slowly fades.

BUT FEW HUMANS HEARD THE WORDS OF THE OCEAN—TO MOST IT WAS NOTHING MORE THAN THE CRASHING OF DISTANT WAVES, THE MURMUR OF A SLOW CREEK, THE MUTED STATIC OF RAINDROPS FALLING UPON WET EARTH. ONLY A FEW, KEEN OF EAR AND PURE OF SOUL, HEARD THE WORDS OF THE OCEAN.

15

You don't believe any of this, do you?

Do you really think that I think the St. Andrew Valley water tower is the all-powerful, all-seeing ruler of all-that-is? Let me ask you something. Do you think every single person sitting in, say, your local church (or temple or mosque or coven or whatever the hell it is your parents drag you to) believes everything they hear? What about the guy who goes to church on Sunday but cheats on his taxes. That's a sin, right? If he truly believed in God, would he sin?

But that doesn't mean the tax cheat isn't religious. Religious is a whole different kettle of fish, as my grandmother would say. *I'm* religious. And I'm *serious*. Serious as a heart attack (Grandma again). Chutengodianism is important to me. But that doesn't mean I think that a big steel tank propped up on a few I-beams is omnipotent. I might be a religious zealot, but I'm not crazy.

So, you ask, how can Jason Bock be serious about a religion that worships a false god?

Are you kidding?

You ever watch a football game and get totally into it? *Why?* It's not a *real* battle. It's just a game somebody made up. So how can you take it seriously? Or, you ever see a movie that made your heart about jump out of your chest? Or one that made you cry? *Why?* It wasn't real. You ever look at a photo of food that made your mouth water? *Why?* You can't eat the picture.

Ah, you say, but the food that the picture shows *is* real. Is it really? Maybe that tasty-looking apple is made of wax. Maybe that loaf of bread is plastic. Maybe the football game is fixed. Maybe the movie is nothing but computer-generated pixels. So it's not as if the picture shows you reality. What you see is somebody's *idea* of reality.

Same thing with water towers and God. I don't have to be a believer to be serious about my religion.

Like any serious Kahuna, I want a well-organized and contented congregation, so I call an official meeting for noon on Tuesday the Sabbath. And like a lying politician, I tell everybody something different to get them there.

Dan is easy. I just tell him it's an official meeting: Be there. Dan was brought up to respect authority figures. I tell Magda that we are planning an ascent of the tower, and I promise to buy Henry a Magnum Brainblaster. As for Shin, all I have to do is tell him that the Ten-legged One has ordered us to gather.

I do not expect things to go all that smoothly. Dan and Shin don't yet know that Henry Stagg is our High Priest. I'm not too worried about Dan, but Shin might freak out when he hears. I decide to treat Henry's induction into the church as a done deal, which it is, and not open it to discussion.

It's a brutally hot day; Wigglesworth's is crowded and noisy with people sucking down a variety of icy beverages. I find the First Keeper, the First Acolyte, and the High Priestess sitting in the big back booth. Magda is chatting away. She has Dan and Shin hypnotized; they're mooning at her like two dogs looking at a bag of treats. I slide in next to her.

"Where's the High Priest?" I ask.

"Haven't seen him," Magda says.

Shin and Dan give me puzzled looks.

"I'm sure he'll be here soon," I say.

Dan says, "What High Priest?"

"Henry."

"Henry *Stagg*?"

I nod.

"Since when?" asks Shin.

"Since the day before yesterday."

Nobody says anything.

I say, "He showed me how to climb the Ten-legged One. I had to make him High Priest."

Shin is giving me a stricken look, but I won't meet his eyes.

I say, "He's not such a bad guy."

Shin says, "He hates me."

"No he doesn't."

"He's *evil*," says Shin.

Magda says, "Maybe if we were all nicer to him, he'd change."

"I don't think you can change a guy like Henry," Dan says.

"Well, I think he has potential," says Magda.

I shrug. "Whatever—he's a Chutengodian now."

"Speak of the devil," Dan says in a low voice.

We all turn to see Henry approaching. He is wearing his usual jeans and boots, and a T-shirt from a rock band called Suicidal Tendencies. He stops a few feet away and looks us over suspiciously.

"This is it?" he says. "I thought you guys'd be dressed up in robes or something."

"We're quite informal," I say.

"Is this everybody? I thought there'd be more."

"We're still seeking new members."

"What about Mitch and Marsh?" Henry says. "I bet they'd join up. Bobby too."

"Those guys?" Dan makes a sour face.

"I'm not sure they'd fit in," I say.

"What's that supposed to mean?" Henry asks.

"They're morons," Shin says. "In case you hadn't noticed."

Henry turns on Shin, his face tight. For a moment I'm afraid he's going to go Neanderthal, and I tense up, ready to jump between them. But Henry freezes, then his knotted face loosens into a grin.

"Since when does being a moron disqualify a guy from worshipping a water tower?" he asks.

"When the church elders say so," I say.

"Isn't that antimoron?"

"I'm afraid it is. Chutengodians discriminate against morons, terrorists, and intelligent fish."

"Who are the church elders?"

"You're looking at them."

Henry shrugs and slides into the booth next to Dan. "Whatever," he says. "I just hope we don't get in trouble for fish discrimination."

I'm surprised by how different Henry seems. This is not the sadistic, dangerous Henry who punched me in the face. It is not the serious, bookish Henry who talks about sci-fi novels. It is not the confident, tower-scaling Henry. This Henry is outnumbered, a little suspicious, and he wants us to like him.

Shin is still giving him a weird stare. Henry notices, but chooses to ignore it.

"Okay," I say. "We're here today to talk about tonight's Midnight Mass. . . . What is it, Magda?"

"If it's at midnight, wouldn't it actually be *tomorrow's* Midnight Mass?" Magda is giving me an innocent, supposedly confused look. Because she is sitting next to me, her face is only about twelve inches from mine.

I say, "What I meant was, the Midnight Mass that is to take place at midnight during the period of darkness which will begin tonight and last until tomorrow morning."

"That's what I thought," she says, grinning.

"We're talking about tonight, though, right?" says Dan.

"Yes," I say. "At midnight. The next midnight there is."

"Tonight," says Henry.

"That's right. The High Priestess was making a technical point."

"We're going up tonight then," says Henry. "All five of us."

"That's right."

Henry looks at Magda. "You going up too?"

Magda raises her eyebrows, making her big eyes even bigger. "You got a problem with that?"

"Not me. I just never met a girl that could climb."

"You have now."

"What about Schinner?" Henry says, looking at me. "He doesn't look like he could climb on a bus, let alone a water tower."

Shin opens his mouth.

"We're all going up," I say, intercepting whatever was about to come out of Shin's mouth.

Henry laughs. "Whatever you say, Your Holiness."

"Please, I prefer to be addressed as 'Your Kahunaness.'"

"Okay, Kahunaness. I'll be there at midnight.

Anybody wants to come up is welcome."

"What are we going to do once we get up there?"
Magda asks.

"Midnight Mass," I say. "Henry, our High Priest, is
going to lead us in worship of the Ten-legged One."

"I am?"

"Sure. That's what High Priests do."

"Not this High Priest."

"It's really easy, Henry. You just talk. Like, 'Blessed
are the climbers: for theirs is the kingdom of water.
Blessed are those who reek: for they shall be cleansed.
Blessed are they who thirst: for they shall drink the
water of life. . . .' Like that."

Not exactly the Sermon on the Mount, but they seem
impressed. Except for Shin, who is still busy sending
thought daggers in Henry's direction.

"That sounded pretty good. Blasphemous, but good,"
says Magda. "I think *you* should lead the mass, Jason."

"That's fine with me," Henry says.

"I thought you wanted to be High Priest."

"You *made* me High Priest. I never said I'd run your
religious service."

Shin suddenly slides out of the booth, his lips working silently, his eyes glistening. He moves quickly
toward the door in his jerky, high-elbowed gait.

"See ya tonight, Schinner," Henry calls after him. He
turns back to us. "What's his problem?"

"Is he okay?" Magda asks.

"He'll be all right," I say, hoping it's true.

"He's one weird dude," Henry says. "Look how he walks. Like he's trying to hold a golfball between his butt cheeks."

Dan and I laugh, but Magda doesn't think it's funny.

"You guys are mean," she says.

Maybe she's right. I shouldn't have laughed. I don't blame Shin for being angry. I should have talked to him before making Henry a Chutengodian.

"You think we should go after him?" Dan says.

"Better not," I say. I hate having to explain and defend Shin's behavior. "I'll talk to him later." We need a change of subject. I slam my fist on the table. "Right now, I thirst! Brainblasters for everybody!"

"You buying?" says Dan.

"This round is on the CTG," I say. "The church coffers will provide!"

"The church has money?" Magda says.

"We will as soon as we take up a collection." I take off my baseball cap and set it upside down on the table. "Who's going to be the first to make a contribution?"

Nobody says anything for a couple of seconds, then Henry makes a suggestion.

"You are," he says.

I was afraid of that. I put my cap back on my head and trudge up to the counter to buy the drinks.

The responsibilities of a religious leader are many and varied.

And expensive.

ND THEY LOOKED UP AND THEY SAW THE GREAT
SILVER BELLY, FAT AND WET, AND THEY FELL
DOWN UPON THEIR KNEES ON THE MOIST EARTH AND
THEY BOWED DOWN BEFORE IT AND THEY NAMED IT
THE TEN-LEGGED GOD.

16

I'm knocking on Shin's window. I
know he's in there, but his blinds are closed and he's not
answering.

It's supposed to hit 100 degrees this afternoon. Feels
like it's there already. The sun is cooking my back and
I'm oozing sweat from every pore. I walk around the
house to the front door and press the bell thirty or forty
times, hoping to irritate him into answering. No luck. I
try the doorknob. It's unlocked. I let myself in, out of the
heat.

Ah, air conditioning! How did people survive without
it? I stand in the Schinners' living room holding my
arms out, letting my body cool and looking around at
the books. Books everywhere. Shin's parents both teach
at Harker College, twenty-five miles away. They are

insane for books. Every possible square foot of wall space is taken up by bookshelves, every shelf stacked two or three deep with volumes of every shape, size, and description. It feels like being in a library where there is no librarian, and nobody throws anything out—not ever.

After I cool off a degree or two, I make my way to the back bedroom, where I find Shin lying flat on his back on his bed, staring at the ceiling. There is a nasty smell in the room, a cross between dead fish and gym socks.

"Hey," I say. "What reeks?"

"You," he replies.

I sit down on the foot of his bed.

"I'm sorry. I should have talked to you."

"Go to hell."

"There is no Chutengodian hell," I say, hoping to get a grin out of him.

No sale. He won't even look at me.

"Look, Shin, I had to let Henry in the church. He wouldn't tell me how to climb the tower unless I let him join." Was that actually true? Maybe not. Another holy lie for the greater good.

"You didn't have to make him High Priest."

"It's just a title. You heard him—he doesn't even want the job."

Shin says nothing.

"You're coming up with us tonight, aren't you?"

"He's not even serious," Shin says, sitting up and wrapping his arms around his knees. "It's just a joke to him."

"What do you expect? I mean, it *is* kind of a joke."

"You better hope *he* doesn't hear you say that."

"Who? Henry?"

Shin gives me a red-eyed look. "Not *Henry*. What do I care what *Henry* thinks? I'm talking about the Ten-legged One."

"Oh." Is he kidding? Once again, I'm not sure. Shin starts rocking back and forth. I hate it when he does that.

I stand up, looking around for a change of subject, and see his gastropodarium. "So, how are your slimers doing?" I peer into the glass tank. "Your little pond is all dried up." My nose wrinkles at the fetid odor. "So this is what reeks!"

"I've been busy."

None of the snails are moving. I reach in and nudge one. It tips over on its side.

"I think they're dead."

"They're not dead," Shin says. "They're estivating."

"What's that?"

"It's what pods do when things get bad. They pull into their shells and cover the opening with a cap of dried mucus. And wait. They can survive for months, waiting for rain." Shin grips his knees with his thin fingers and leans forward, his eyes shimmering. "Wouldn't that be great?"

"You want me to give them some water?"

"Leave 'em alone."

"I think some of them are dead, Shin."

"I don't care."

"You don't care if they die?"

He shrugs.

I feel bad for the snails. Shin is their god, and he has abandoned them. "I think you should come up with us tonight," I say.

He shakes his head. "Henry was right about one thing. There's no way I can climb that leg."

"You won't have to."

"Oh? You going to build me an elevator?"

"I'm gonna build us a stairway to heaven."

My mother has decided I have a hearing problem.

"I've been calling you for five minutes, Jason!"

"I was in the garage, Mom. Gimme a break."

"What were you doing in the garage? My God, you're dripping sweat! Aren't you feeling well?"

"It's one hundred and twenty degrees out there, Mom. Anybody would sweat."

"What on earth were you doing?"

"Working on a project."

"What project?"

"It's a religious thing, Mom."

"Oh! Something for your TPO group?"

"Something like that. What did you want?"

"To tell you I've made an appointment for you at the clinic."

"What for?"

"Your annual blood screening."

"Mom, I just had a blood test. I'm not even sick."

"I know that dear, but we don't want to take any chances now, do we?"

After a lifetime of this, I've learned not to bother arguing. It's easier to give up a few tubes of blood.

I am in my bedroom at my desk working on a drawing of Magda, Goddess of Love, when my dad knocks on my door.

"Anybody home?"

I shove the Goddess of Love under some other papers.

"C'mon in."

He pushes open the door and looks around my room with a nervous frown, as if he's afraid he might find a python curled up on the bed, or a pound of heroin, or a dead body.

When none of the above appear, he smiles. "How's it going, Jay?"

"Okay," I say.

He sits down on the edge of my unmade bed. "Mom tells me you've been working on some sort of project for church."

"Oh. Well, I was, but it didn't work out."

"What were you making? Maybe I can help."

"It's no big deal."

"You sure?"

"Yeah."

We look at each other for a long time, maybe two seconds.

"So!" my father claps his hands on his knees. "How's it going with the TPO?"

"I go to the meetings. Some of the kids are all right."

"I hear you talk about quite a number of different things."

"We talk about whatever," I say, wondering where this is going.

"I bet you kids come up with some pretty wild stuff."

"Not really."

"When I was your age, I had some pretty strange ideas."

"Really? Like what?"

"When I was in college I questioned my faith," he says, shaking his head as if such a thing were almost too bizarre to be believed.

I wonder what would happen if I told him I was a Chutengodian. He'd probably send me to a Catholic military academy, or have me committed. An alarming thought occurs to me.

"Have you been talking to Just Al?" I ask.

He looks puzzled.

"I mean, Al Anderson," I say.

"Oh. Actually, I did run into Al this morning over at Good Shepherd."

I say, "You know, we have a pact at the TPO meetings. Everything we say in those meetings is private, just like what you say in the confessional. What did Al tell you?"

My father shifts his feet and licks his lips the way he does when he wishes he were somewhere else.

"Nothing. He was just saying that you kids have a lot of strange ideas, that's all."

"Well I think that sucks. I don't know how he expects us to be open and honest when he's going to repeat everything we say to our parents."

"Now calm down, Jay. It wasn't anything like that."

"Then what *did* he say?"

"He told me that a lot of pretty radical ideas get tossed around in those meetings. I asked him to give me an example. He told me about this one kid who's invented his own god called the Ten-legged something-or-other. We had a good laugh about that. Then I asked him how you were doing, and he said, 'Why don't you ask him?' So that's what I'm doing. It's not like he handed me a transcript, Jay."

"Still, he shouldn't be saying anything."

"Maybe not, Jay." He stands up and claps me on the shoulder. "But I'm glad to hear you're doing so well."

"Me too," I say.

After he leaves, closing the door behind him, I pull out the Goddess of Love and get back to work.

AND SO IT CAME TO BE THAT A GROUP OF DISCIPLES SET FORTH TO SPREAD THE WORD OF THE TEN-LEGGED ONE THROUGHOUT THE LAND, AND THEY CALLED THEMSELVES CHUTENGODIANS, AND FOR A TIME THE OCEAN WAS CONTENT.

17

I watch the worshippers arrive.

First there is Dan, who shows up a predictable ten minutes early. He strolls up the slope, tips his head back to gaze upward at the majesty of the Ten-legged One, then sits down on one of the leg bases to wait. He does not see me.

A few minutes later, Magda and Henry arrive together. Henry is carrying a large backpack. Magda is dressed in black jeans and a halter top. Having recently drawn a picture of her wearing far less than that, I feel as if I can see right through her clothing. Interesting. But why is she with Henry? Maybe they ran into each other—they both live on the same side of town. Dan sees them and walks over. I can't hear what they say.

At exactly midnight, they are looking around, probably wondering where I am. They move closer and I hear Dan say, "He probably went to get Shin." Henry says something in a low voice and Magda laughs. I feel myself clench up. I don't know what Henry said, but I don't like that Magda thought it was funny.

"I'm hot," Magda complains. "It must still be in the eighties."

"I bet it's in the nineties," says Dan.

They are right underneath me now.

"We might as well go up," Henry says. "There'll be a nice breeze up top."

"How do we do it?" asks Dan.

"Piece a cake. I'll show you."

Magda says, "Let's wait a couple minutes. I'm sure they'll be here."

"They can get up on their own. Jay knows how."

"It'll be more fun if we all go up together."

I see a ghostly, pale figure approaching from the south, moving slowly, dejectedly, like a man walking to his own funeral. Shin.

"You guys can wait," Henry says. "I'm going up." He starts for the leg.

"Hold on a sec, Henry," I say.

Henry jumps like he's been goosed, looking around wildly for the source of my voice.

"I'm up here," I say.

They all look up and find me sitting cross-legged on the small landing at the bottom of the spiral staircase.

Shin stops a few yards behind them. He is wearing his X-men pajamas.

"How'd you get up there?" Magda asks.

"I flew."

"Is Shin with you?" Dan asks.

"He's right behind you."

They turn and look.

Henry says, "What's that you got on, Schinner?" He laughs. "Are those pajamas?"

"The First Keeper of the Sacred text," Shin says, "can wear whatever the hell he wants."

"Oh yeah? What if the High Priest has a problem with that?"

I don't want this to go any further, so I yell, "Look out below!" They all jump back and I shove the rope ladder off the landing. It clatters and flops and swings back and forth: a fourteen-foot-long rope ladder with wooden rungs, constructed in my garage only hours ago.

"The Ten-legged One wishes you all to climb in comfort and safety," I say.

Henry gives the ladder a tug. "You think this thing will hold?"

"I guarantee it."

"It's cheating."

"If you don't want to use it, you don't have to."

"I don't, and I won't," says Henry, turning his back and heading for the leg. "Anybody wants to come up the *real* way, follow me." He starts up, climbing the leg almost as quickly as a normal person would walk up a staircase. It doesn't surprise me that Henry rejected my ladder. He wants to show off his monkey genes.

"Look at him go!" Dan says, impressed. "Is that how you got up?" he asks me.

"Yep." I don't mention that it took me twenty minutes, with numerous rest stops on the way.

"I don't think I could do that," Magda says.

"Be sure to tell Henry that. It'll give him a thrill. Now, which of you will be attending mass this evening?"

Magda surprises me by coming up the ladder first.

"I don't think I can get past you," she says.

I want to wait and make sure that Shin makes it up, so I swing to the outside of the staircase to make room. "Go ahead," I say.

Magda starts up the staircase.

Dan says, "You going, Shin?"

"I want to be last."

Dan shrugs, climbs up, and squeezes past me. Magda is a quarter of the way up. Henry has already reached the lower catwalk.

Shin grabs the ladder and puts his right foot on the lowest rung. He hesitates.

"C'mon, Shin. It's just like walking up the steps at school."

He climbs the ladder carefully, testing each rung before putting his full weight on it. I look up. Magda and Henry are already on the upper catwalk, looking down at us.

"You guys okay?" Magda shouts.

I wave, telling her we are fine. Shin is at the top of the ladder.

"You want to squeeze past me?" I say.

"No," he says. "You go first." He sounds a little shaky.

"Whatever you say." I start up the steps, moving slowly and looking back every few seconds. Shin is following me, but he's having a hard time, hanging onto the railing with both hands. It's not a matter of strength or coordination. He's just flat-out petrified.

"Just don't look down," I say, echoing Henry's advice to me.

It was the wrong thing to say.

I arrive at the top to find Dan clinging to the light post (red flash), Magda sitting with her back to the ladder railing (flash), and Henry hunched over the hatch with his arm pumping back and forth (flash), sweat glistening on his arms and neck, making a scraping, grinding noise. It's maybe a couple of degrees cooler on top, but still pretty warm. The steel top of the tank is radiating residual heat from the sun.

Magda looks down the ladder. "Where's Shin?"

"He's stuck," I say. "Hey Henry, what're you doing?"

"Sawing," Henry says.

"Is he okay?" Magda asks.

"Shin? Not really. About a third of the way up the leg he froze."

Dan says, "What's his problem?"

"I think he's afraid of heights. He'll be okay."

Magda says, "You just left him there?"

"He told me to go on up. He said he wanted me to leave him alone a while." I look again at Henry. "What are you sawing?"

"I'm going down to talk to him." Magda heads down the ladder.

Some Head Kahuna I am, leaving my High Priestess to deal with my wayward Keeper. But the fact is, I am furious with Shin. I went to all the trouble of making that ladder for him, and he freezes up on me. It's embarrassing! As far as I'm concerned, he can stay there the rest of the night.

"That flashing light is driving me nuts," I say.

"I'll fix it," Henry says. "Look out, Danny-boy." Dan lets go of the light post and grabs for the railing just as Henry swings something at the light. The bulb shatters with a loud pop, sending shards of red glass sliding off the tank in all directions.

"Are you *crazy*?" Dan yells, his voice cracking.

Henry is laughing. I notice that the thing in his hand is a hacksaw.

"That's an aviation warning light. Now an airplane could hit us," Dan says.

"When's the last time you saw an airplane fly this low over St. Andrew Valley?" Henry says. He goes back to his sawing. "Besides, I like the dark."

It *is* nice to be rid of the flashing beacon. Our light now comes from the three-quarter moon rising in the east. The top of the tank is shimmering silver. We are standing atop the planet of the Ten-legged One. . . . Wait a sec, what is Henry doing with a hacksaw?

"What are you doing?" I ask.

He leans to the side to show me. He is sawing through the padlock that holds the hatch closed. "Brain surgery," he says with a grin.

18

"You can't do that!" Dan says.

"Sure I can. Look. I'm doing it." Just as Henry says that, the saw blade snaps.

"I guess the Ten-legged One does not desire brain surgery," I say.

"I got it almost sawed through." Henry swings the broken hacksaw at the lock, whacking it repeatedly. The sound of the saw banging against the hatch echoes beneath our feet; I can feel the vibration. He gives it one last hard blow, getting his whole body behind it, and the lock snaps off, skids a few feet, nearly stops, then picks up speed as the slope of the tank steepens. As the lock disappears over the horizon, I'm reminded of how near we are to death.

A second later we hear a loud metallic *bonk,* then an angry shout.

"Who was that?" Dan asks.

"Sounded like Magda," Henry says.

"I better go see if she's okay," I say, starting down the ladder.

I meet Magda on the catwalk.

"What *was* that?" she asks. "It almost hit me!"

"Henry cut the padlock off the hatch."

"Why?"

"I don't know. I don't know why Henry does any of the things he does." I look over the railing. "Is Shin still down there?"

"I didn't see him."

"He didn't fall, I hope."

"I went all the way down. I didn't see him anywhere. He must've climbed down and gone home."

"Oh." Shin must be miserable. He was so hard on himself the first time he tried and failed to climb the tower; this time must be even worse. I imagine how he must be feeling. Not good. I consider going after him . . . but what good would that do? I can't change him. He is who he is. I can't be responsible for every little glitch in his pathetic life.

"He's a funny guy."

"I feel bad for him."

"Yeah, me too." I try to recapture some of the bad feeling so that I can share this feel-bad-moment with Magda, but mostly I'm just mad at Shin for being such a wuss. How did I end up with a best friend who raises snails, anyway? I refuse to let Shin's weirdness interfere with my social life. Or my religion.

"We'd better find out what Henry's up to," I say.

We climb back up. Henry has the hatch open. He and Dan are peering into the opening.

"Shin went home," I say.

Henry says, "I told you he wouldn't make it. I don't know why you bother with him."

"He's my friend," I say, transferring some of my anger from Shin to Henry.

"That doesn't make him less of a loser. Grab my backpack for me, would ya?"

I push Henry's backpack over to him with my foot. He digs inside and comes out with a flashlight. He aims the beam down into the hatch.

"What do you see?"

"A platform."

Magda and I look past Henry and Dan's heads at a steel grating about seven feet below the hatch. Henry sticks his head and arm deep inside, casting about with the beam of light.

"Anybody home?" His voice echoes weirdly.

Magda asks, "Can you see the water?"

"Yeah . . . it's about ten feet below the platform. Here, hold this." He hands the flashlight up to Dan.

Next thing I know, Henry's in the tank.

"Gimme the light," he says. Dan lowers the flashlight in to Henry, who is standing on the steel platform.

"What do you see?"

"It's nice and cool in here."

"You better come out of there, Henry," I say.

"No way! Hey, there's, like, a chain thing here. Lemme . . ." A scraping clanking noise echoes up from the hatch. "You can't believe how rusty this thing is."

"What's he doing?" I ask Dan.

"I don't know."

There is a sudden rattling and a splash.

"What happened? Is he okay?"

"He just dropped something into the water," Dan says.

"It's a chain ladder, you guys," Henry shouts. "Hey Danny, grab these, would ya?"

Dan reaches in and comes out with Henry's cowboy boots. "Take these, too." Henry hands up his socks. Dan wrinkles his nose and stuffs the socks into the boots.

"What's he doing now?" Magda asks.

"He's—oh my god—"

The sound of a loud splash up through the hatch, followed by a shouted "Yee-ha!"

"He jumped in," Dan says.

"Whooo-eee!" screams Henry. "Check it out!"

"Omigod, let me see!" says Magda, shoving Dan aside and dipping her head into the hatch. "Henry? You okay?"

"This is *awesome*. Come on in!"

She lifts her head up and says, "He wants us to go swimming."

I shout into the hatch, "Henry! We came up here for Midnight Mass, not swimming!"

"Screw the mass! It's baptism time!"

"I know one thing for sure," I say. "I'm not drinking any tap water for the next few days."

People will surprise you. You just don't know for sure what anybody's going to do. For example, I never would have guessed that both Dan and Magda would climb into that tank and jump into the water. And I never would've guessed that Magda would be the first, stripping down to her dark panties and pink bra right there in front of us and jumping into the cold water with a blood-curdling shriek. Dan followed her in almost immediately, only he kept his shorts on.

Me? I'm alone on the Godhead, standing in the center of a great steel ball with nothing but a broken light, a pile of clothing, and Henry Stagg's cowboy boots for company. Muffled shouts and screams and laughter echo up through the open hatch. A warm breeze ruffles my hair.

I think it is totally crazy what they are doing. What if that rusty chain ladder isn't strong enough to hold them? They'd swim around in circles until they drowned. And what if we got caught polluting the city water with our sweaty, unwashed bodies? We might get thrown in jail.

No, it's completely crazy, irresponsible, dangerous, and immature. I look around at St. Andrew Valley, at all the houses filled with sleeping, unsuspecting citizens. What would they think if they knew what was going on up here? I imagine John Q. Citizen waking up in the middle of the night and pouring himself a glass of tap water. *Hmm. Tastes like unwashed teenage bodies. Must be having a bad dream.*

I lower myself through the hatch. Cool, moist air surrounds me. The flashlight is on the platform, its beam lighting up the great curved wall of the tank. I point it down and scan the surface until I find Magda's dark head bobbing in the water.

"C'mon, in, Jason!" she shouts.

I swing the beam of the light around, marveling at the size of the tank. It seems bigger on the inside than it does on the outside.

"Hey Kahuna, you coming in or not?" There's Henry, doing a backstroke. Dan is a few yards away, treading water.

People will surprise you. You never know what dumbass thing they're going to do next. I pull off my shoes and toss them up through the hatch. I take off my socks and my T-shirt, but leave my jeans on because I've got holes in my underwear. I hang my legs out over the edge of the platform, take a breath, and push off into space.

Sometimes even I surprise me.

The shock of hitting the cold water sends the breath rushing from my lungs. I kick and dig with my arms, making for the surface. It can't be more than a second, but it feels like forever before I break through and suck in a fresh lungful of oxygen. But something is wrong. It's black. The blackest black I've ever been in, blacker than closed eyes in bed at night.

I've gone blind.

"Hey!" I shout. "You guys here? I can't see!"

"Of course you can't, you dumb ass!" Henry's voice. "You knocked the flashlight into the water when you jumped."

"Oh," I say.

"Where are you guys?" Dan's voice.

"Over here," Magda says.

"Over where?" I say. The darkness seems to amplify the echoes. I can't tell what direction the voices are coming from.

"That was a really stupid move, your Kahunaness," says Henry.

"Sorry. Can anybody see anything at all?"

Dan says, "How are we gonna find the ladder?"

"It's right in the middle."

"Yeah, but where's the middle?"

"It must be close to where you jumped in, Kahunaness."

Magda, off to my left, says, "I think I see the hatch."

"Where are you?"

"Over here. Up against the wall."

"If you swim toward it, you might run into the ladder."

Dan says, "I'm getting tired."

"Try floating."

"I don't float."

"Magda? Are you swimming toward the hatch?"

"I'm—"

Something hits me hard in the eye.

"Ow! Who was that?"

"Sorry!" Magda says. "You were in my way. I can't see the hatch anymore. You can only see it when you're up against the wall, otherwise the platform blocks it."

I can't see her, but I hear her breathing. I sense her body just a couple of feet away.

Henry says, "If everybody just swims around for awhile, one of us is bound to run into the ladder."

I say, "I got an idea. We make a human chain. We hold hands and swim across the tank till we hit the ladder."

"Sounds good to me," Dan says. He is breathing hard. "Where are you?"

"I'm over here," says Magda.

"Keep talking."

"Henry? You coming?"

"Right here." His voice is surprisingly close.

"Okay. Dan?"

"I can't find you."

"Keep following my voice."

The sound of his splashing gets closer, then we hear a squeal from Magda.

"Hey, keep your hands where they belong!"

"Sorry!"

"We all here? Let's grab hands."

I reach out, touching Magda's shoulder, then sliding my hand down along her arm to her hand. On my other side, Henry is groping at me. We manage to clasp hands. My legs are churning double-time to stay afloat.

"You got hold of Dan over there, Magda?"

"I got him. Now what?"

"Now we start swimming, keeping our hands clasped and our arms stretched out."

"How do we—*urk*!"

"What the—hey, we all gotta be facing the same way." Two very confusing minutes later, our human chain is relinked. We start swimming backward, propelled by eight kicking feet. Henry and Dan, on the ends, add some arm action. I figure our chain is almost twenty feet long. The tank is about seventy feet across.

"How do you know we're going the right way?" Dan asks.

"I don't. But if we just keep going till we hit the wall, then we can see the hatch. We swim for the hatch then, we're bound to run into the ladder."

It's a good plan.

I wonder if it will work.

19

Three times we reached the smooth metal wall of the tank, and three times we launched ourselves back toward the center of the tank, only to end up running into the wall again. How could we be missing the ladder? I don't know how long we can keep swimming. I'm getting tired, and Dan is breathing so loud I'm afraid he's going to panic. Then it occurs to me that Henry and I are probably stronger swimmers than Magda and Dan, causing our human chain to swing off to one side.

"Ease up a little, Henry," I say as we push off the wall for the third time. We kick our way through darkness. What if the chain ladder fell into the water with the flashlight? We would swim blindly until, one by one, we sink into the waters, never to be found until the citizens of St. Andrew Valley complain of a nasty, rotten flavor in their drinking water and—

—something whacks the top of my head, and I hear the rattle of rusty chain. I've found the ladder with my head.

We send Magda up first. She is the lightest, and the least likely to break the rusted ladder. Once she's up, Henry follows, then Dan, then me, the Big Kahuna. The ladder holds up admirably. I emerge from the hatch with a sense of giddy relief. I have survived being devoured by a god. I am Jonah, spat out by the whale.

Around me, the Chutengodians are getting dressed. Magda is talking rapid-fire, spewing out her excitement in the form of words.

"I thought we were gonna be in there till we drowned or something. My god, that was so *crazy*." She pulls her jeans up over her slim hips. "Henry, you're crazy, you know that? What if that ladder had broken? What if somebody had climbed up and closed the hatch on us?"

Henry, shirtless, is standing on one leg struggling to pull on a cowboy boot. "Who'd do that? Schinner? He's too scared to climb up here."

I realize that I haven't thought about Shin for one second since we went into the tank.

Dan says, "I wish we'd brought up some sodas or something. I'm thirsty."

"You just spent half an hour floating around in a million gallons of drinking water!"

"I wasn't thirsty then," says Dan.

Henry is working on his other boot, hopping up and down on his left foot, tugging at the loops on either side of his right boot.

"Careful," I say. "It's slippery up here with all this water."

Just then Henry's heel comes down on a wet spot and his foot skids out from under him and he falls, flat on his back, feet splayed out toward the horizon.

Dan and I both start to laugh, then stifle it as we realize that Henry might be in trouble. He rolls over onto his belly and tries to crawl toward us, but he's too far out on the slope. He slides one knee forward but the movement causes him to slip down another two inches. His fingers scrabble on the steel surface, but there's nothing there to grab. Spread-eagled on his bare belly, he looks up at us with wide, terrified eyes. I think the suction between his belly and the smooth steel of the tank is the only thing holding him.

"Help me," he says in a small voice.

I shake off the momentary paralysis. "Dan, grab hold of the light post!" I say. Dan grasps the post with both hands, I take hold of Dan's ankle with one hand and, on my belly now, stretch my other hand out to Henry. It's too far.

"I'm coming," says Magda. I feel her clamber over me; she's holding onto my arm and I'm holding onto her as she stretches her feet toward Henry. He should be able to reach her, but as he lifts his hand to grab for her ankle he suddenly slides down another foot.

"Grab my ankle, Henry!" Magda shouts, but she can't see how far down he has slid. I watch, helpless, as Henry slowly slides over the horizon, his naked belly squeaking against metal.

"Oh, shit," I hear him say just before he disappears from sight.

Henry does not scream as he falls. I would have. But Henry falls silently, at least for a second, then we hear a loud *clang*.

Did he hit the ground so quickly? No, *that* sound wouldn't be so loud and close and metallic-sounding. He must've bounced off a leg on his way down. These thoughts tumble through my mind in a fraction of a second. Then comes the scream, but it's not from Henry.

"Henryyyyyy!" Magda shrieks, her voice so high and loud I can feel it all the way to the center of my brain.

"Did he fall?" Dan asks.

"He's gone," I say.

A wordless, sobbing wail comes from Magda.

I start to pull her back up to safety. She is dead weight. "Come on, Magda. I can't hold you much longer."

Slowly, Magda crawls back over me, sobbing hysterically. I want to sob hysterically too, but a part of me— the Kahuna part—knows that we have to pull ourselves together before we can afford to fall apart. Magda makes it back to the railing. I am climbing back, holding onto Dan, when we hear a weird moan.

My first thought is that it's the tower speaking to us. But it's not coming from within the tank, but from outside.

Magda is the first to realize what it is.

She shouts, "Henry!"

Henry's quavering voice slides up over the tank. "I think I busted my leg."

"Omigod, he's alive!" Magda says. She grabs me, wrapping her arms around my middle and squeezing. "He's *alive!*" Is she hugging me or Henry? I am confused. How could Henry have survived a two-hundred-foot fall? And why can we hear him so clearly?

"He must have landed on the catwalk," Dan says.

Of course. The catwalk that circles the tank sticks out about three feet, and it's only thirty feet below us. Henry must have been able to slow himself down enough so that he dropped straight down the side of the tank to land on the catwalk.

"Are you all right?" Magda calls out.

"No!"

"We better go help him," I say. Dan is already headed down the ladder. I grab Henry's backpack and look at Magda. She is smiling joyfully, her eyes wet with tears. "He's *alive,*" she says.

"Yeah, he's alive." I'm alive too, I think. Would she smile that hard for me? "Let's go get him."

Henry is lying on the catwalk with one leg stretched out in front of him and the other jutting out at an angle that makes me want to throw up. His thigh is broken. He looks like he has two knees on one leg. His face is white and knotted with pain. He is breathing rapidly, like a dog panting.

"Good one, Henry," I say.

He stares at me, but does not reply. I look up at the wall of the tank and imagine what it must have been like for him, going over the edge of the planet like that. Was he hoping to hit the catwalk? Did he even remember the catwalk was there? Or did his mind go completely blank with fear?

Magda is bent over him, cradling his head.

Dan says, "We gotta get him down. How are we gonna get him down?"

I look over the railing, down at the ground, and suddenly I am blinded by a brilliant white light. The light plays across the tank, leaving us in momentary darkness, then returns, holding steady.

An amplified voice rings out, "You on the water tower, come on down now."

Dan says again, "How are we gonna get him down?"

"I think that's going to be somebody else's problem," I say.

20

I cannot recommend jail, unless you enjoy misery, fear, loneliness, and the sounds and smells of a drunk puking in the next cell. Also, I think I might have picked up a flea infestation. My head itches like crazy.

I am *Bock. J. Bock.* Radical Religious Zealot. Leader of the Chutengodian Jihad. Mastermind of the Terrorist Assassins, Captured in the Act of Poisoning the Water Supply with sweat, spit, and one flashlight, imprisoned by godless heathens for crimes against nature. . . .

Forget about it. I'm hungry and scared and I'm gagging at the reek of my neighbor's winey vomit. I lay wide-eyed on the narrow cot, staring at some pink chunky glop stuck to the ceiling. What is it? How did it get up there? My stomach churns.

There are no windows, no clocks. Does that make the time go faster? I don't think so.

A policeman walks past my cell and I say, "Do you know what time it is?"

He stops and looks in at me and says, "Time to think about your life, son."

"Do you know if my friend Henry is all right?"

"I don't know your friend Henry. Was he here?"

"No."

"Then, he's probably better off than you are."

"What about Magda and Dan?"

"Those other two kids? Their parents already picked them up."

"I want to call my dad."

"You already had your phone call."

"Are there fleas in here?" I ask, scratching my head.

He laughs. "Son, there's a lot worse than fleas."

My father lets me rot in jail until almost 9:00 A.M. It's just as well. When he finally bails me out, he is so mad he can't talk. I can't imagine how angry he must have been when he got the 3:00 A.M. phone call from the police.

"You sit in back" is the only thing he says to me.

I get in the backseat of his Buick. His jaw muscle is pulsing so hard I'm afraid he's going to pulverize his molars.

Halfway home, I say, "I'm sorry, Dad."

The frequency of the jaw pulses increases. This is bad. I've never seen him like this.

The first time I climbed the tower with Henry Stagg, we told each other things. I told Henry about my mother's obsession with diseases, and my father's obsession with religion. Henry told me about his father, who used to beat him with a belt.

The belt was black with silver studs. He would fold it over once, drape Henry over his knee and whack him three times with the buckle end for every minute of aggravation Henry had given him. There were times, Henry told me, when his ass oozed blood for a week. Two years ago Henry's father got killed in a truck accident. Henry says he doesn't miss him one bit.

My father has never hit me with anything. But, at this moment, if he happened to have a silver-studded belt in his hands, I'm sure I'd never be able to sit down again.

We get home and go into the house. I walk past my mother, who stares at me as if I'm some sort of freak of nature. I go to my room and shut the door. It feels as if years have passed. I look at my books, my computer, my clothes—none of it seems important anymore, not after last night. Not after nearly drowning, and then watching Henry die, and then finding out he was alive, and the police and the ambulance crew bringing Henry down . . . and the hours sitting in jail, sitting in that bright cell alone with the retching and the foul smells.

I'm hungry, but there is no way I am going out there and facing my mother.

No way.

I think about Magda and Dan. Are they in as much trouble as I am? I don't know anything about Magda's parents, but as for Dan, his Holy Roller father has probably grounded him for the rest of his life.

Shin is lucky he didn't come up with us. I wonder how he is doing. Does he even know what happened? Probably not. He's probably still in bed.

I scour my mind for something to make me feel better. All I can come up with is Paul the Apostle, who was imprisoned repeatedly for his religious activities. Is this how he felt?

I wouldn't have been on top of that tower if it weren't for my religion. Does that make me a martyr? Am I being persecuted?

I wonder how my father will respond to that argument.

Not well, I fear.

A few minutes later I hear determined, fatherly footsteps. He opens my door without knocking.

"Jason, your mother and I would like to talk to you."

He walks away, leaving the door open. I follow him into the living room. My parents are perched stiffly in their matching club chairs. I sit on the sofa, facing them. The prisoner facing his persecutors, waiting to hear the sentence they are about to impose. Will they send me back to jail? Will I spend the rest of my life in a labor camp? Will I be put in stocks in the public square? Will I be drawn and quartered—one limb tied to each of four horses and pulled slowly apart? Will I be whipped and beaten and spat upon and forced to drag a wooden cross to my place of execution?

My father begins with the ritual throat clearing, then speaks.

"Jason, I hardly know what to say. In fact, I'm not even going to bother asking you why you were up there on that water tower. No answer you could possibly give us would be satisfactory. The Stagg boy is in St. Theresa's Hospital, lucky to be alive. You're all lucky to be alive."

I, the accused, say nothing.

"The question now is, what are we going to do with you?"

I maintain my silence.

After a few seconds he says, "Well?"

"I'm sorry, I thought the question was rhetorical."

His eyes bulge, and I immediately regret my comment, even though it was completely true.

"Jason," he says, fighting to keep his voice under control, "do you want to continue to live here with us, under this roof?"

I nod. It's not such a bad place. I try to keep my chin up and look him in the eyes, but it's not so easy, what with all the smoldering and burning and glittering going on there. I shift my gaze down and over to my mother's hands, fingers all over each other like ten jittery worms having a wrestling match. It reminds me of how much my head itches. I start scratching.

"What do *you* think we should do, Jason?" my father says.

"I don't know. I'm not going to be climbing any more water towers."

"Do you think you should be punished?"

"No."

His jaw pulses as he chews on that.

"Your mother and I disagree," he says.

I shrug. The funny thing is, although I'm embarrassed at getting caught, I don't feel all that bad about climbing the Ten-legged One. What's the big deal? Nobody got hurt. Except for Henry, and that was his own fault.

But I know I'm going to pay a price. I'm paying right now with all the itching.

My father clears his throat again.

"Here is what we've decided, Jason. You are not to leave the house except on errands, or to attend TPO meetings, or on other business approved of by your mother and me, until the beginning of school."

That's only six weeks away. I can handle it.

"And no phone privileges."

Uh-oh.

"Furthermore, you will not be getting your drivers' license this fall. That will have to wait until next year."

Ouch! That one really hurts.

"Look, I don't—" I stop talking just in time. Who knows what sort of incriminating declaration was about to come out of my mouth? I certainly don't.

"You don't what?" my father asks, his voice artificially mild.

"Nothing," I say, scratching behind my right ear.

"Why are you scratching?" my mother asks, speaking for the first time.

"I think I got fleas or lice or something," I say.

That ends the meeting fast.

21

After showering and washing my entire body with some sort of insecticide shampoo my mother has been hoarding, I am once again permitted to retire to my cell. I hear my father grousing about how he lost half a day at work over this "teenage idiocy," and my mother scouring the house for cooties with her little handheld vacuum cleaner. By noon, things have calmed down. My father leaves for his office. My mother performs another half hour of frantic cleaning, then knocks on my door to tell me she is going to her bridge club.

As soon as I hear her car roll out of the driveway, I'm on the phone to Shin, partly to find out if he's okay, and partly because I just have to tell him about what happened.

I get the answering machine.

"Shin, it's me. Call me."

My next call is to Magda. Her mother answers.

"Is Magda there?"

"Who is calling, please?"

This is no time to be truthful. "This is Joe Finklemarster."

"Joe who?"

"Uh, Frinkleman . . . ster." *Damn!*

"I'm sorry, but Magda is not taking any telephone calls, Mr. Finklefrinklewhatever. Good-bye."

So much for that. I try calling Dan, but when I get the answering machine I just hang up. They've probably got him in a straightjacket.

I call St. Theresa's Hospital.

"I'm calling for one of your patients—Henry Stagg?"

"Just one moment."

I scratch my head and smell my fingers. Insecticide shampoo smells like insecticide. If I was a flea, I'd leave too.

"Hello?"

"Henry?"

"Jay-boy?"

"How are you doing?"

"Broken femur, two busted ribs, and a dislocated finger."

"Ouch."

"I have to crap in a pan."

"At least you're not dead."

"Yeah, well, dead would be easier."

"How long do you have to be in the hospital?"

"A few days, then I go home. They say I'll be on crutches for a couple months. Hey, I can't remember— did we shut that hatch?"

"I think so."

"Good. Maybe they don't know we were in the tank. The cops were here, but I pretended I was asleep."

"We were all soaking wet, Henry. They know we were in there."

"Oh well, what can they do?"

"We're going to find out."

"I s'pose. It was worth it, though. Wasn't it?"

"I don't know about that."

"Hey, Kahunaness, no matter what they do to you, they aren't gonna break your legs. I'm the only one paying the steep price here, and I say it was worth it."

"I say you're a nutcase." Usually I wouldn't talk to Henry like that, but I figure the broken leg and the fact that he's ten miles away in the hospital give me a safety margin.

"Think about it, Einstein," he says. "You live to be a hundred, you're gonna remember it like it was yesterday. It was probably one of the great moments of your life. Sure, maybe they'll send you to ding-dong school, take away your DVD player, whatever. That's nothing. Who else you know that's swum in a water tower? How long you think it'll be before you have another night you'll never forget? Me, a few months I'll be healed up like nothing ever happened. But I'll still have last night. It was like a religious experience."

"What if you'd missed the catwalk?"

"I'd do it again in a second."

"Henry, are you high on something?"

"They got me on some kind of IV drip. I'm not hurtin', I can tell you that. Hey, y'know what'd be cool? We could haul some inner tubes up, about six flashlights, a boom box . . . get a bunch of girls up there . . ."

"How are you going to climb with your leg all busted up?"

"I'm planning for the future."

Henry Stagg is, of course, certifiably insane. But I do wonder what it would sound like to crank up some Metallica or Eminem inside that enormous metal cavern. If you got it loud enough, maybe people would hear it coming out their faucets.

He's also right about it being an unforgettable experience. I'll never forget swimming in that tank. Of course, I'll never forget the time I got my finger slammed in the car door when I was nine years old, and that's not an experience I'd want to repeat.

I dial Shin's number, but get the machine again. I look at the clock. Two P.M. That gives me two hours before my mother gets home. I decide to go for it. Nobody grounds the pope, so why should I be any different?

22

Shin is sitting at the metal grid table on his patio writing in his sketchbook, eating Oreos, and washing them down with a big glass of water.

"Hey," I say, coming around the side of his house.

He looks up, blinks, and closes the sketchbook. I sit down across from him and grab a cookie.

"We missed you last night," I say, shoving the entire cookie into my mouth.

"I went home," he says, not looking up.

Crunch, crunch, crunch, gulp. That's about all Oreos are good for—three crunches and a gulp. Now, where's that glass of milk?

"The height kind of got to you, huh?"

He glares at me.

I say, "I don't think we're going to be doing much climbing anymore."

Shin says nothing.

"You hear what happened?"

He shakes his head.

"We got caught."

He shrugs.

"And Henry fell off the top of the tower."

Now I've got his attention.

"He landed on the catwalk."

"Is he okay?"

"Yes. I mean, no. He's in the hospital, but he's *going* to be okay."

"How did he fall?" Shin asks. He wraps his hands around his glass of water and takes a reverent sip, like a priest drinking from his chalice.

"He slipped on some water."

"It was wet? It didn't rain last night."

"It got kind of wet after we went swimming."

"You went swimming?"

I can see he doesn't get it.

"We went swimming inside the tank."

Shin blinks, confused.

"Inside the head of the Ten-legged One," I say. "We went swimming. All of us."

Shin's mouth drops open. His eyes go to the glass of water in his hands, his hands relax, the glass falls, bounces on the table, spilling its waters across Shin's lap, and falls off the table's edge to shatter on the flagstones.

✸   ✸   ✸

On the way home I stop and look up at the Ten-legged
One. It stands out against the blue sky with remarkable
clarity. My eyes follow the spiral ladder around and up
the column to the first catwalk, then up to the second
catwalk. I see the spot where Henry landed. I imagine
him sliding off the tank, disappearing over the near
horizon. My stomach clenches and I have to look away.

I will never forget the look on Henry's face as he slid
over the curve of the tank. "Oh, shit," he said, and we
all thought those were his last words. Even Henry must
have thought so.

I wonder what my last words will be. I hope they
won't be "Oh, shit."

I walk toward home in the bright afternoon light. One
thing Henry is right about—it was a night I will never
forget.

I'm afraid Shin will never forget it either.

After I told him we went swimming in the tank, he
got very agitated.

"You entered the Godhead without me?" he said,
standing up.

"We could hardly be *with* you, Shin. You weren't
there."

"I don't care." Pacing back and forth, shards of shattered glass crunching beneath his shoes. "You should've
waited."

"Wait for what? You took off."

"I'm still going up there."

"Shin . . ."

"I have to go." He gave me his most reasonable look. "I've received instructions from on high."

"Look, Shin, you think maybe we're getting too serious with this Ten-legged God business?"

"What do you mean?"

"I mean, fun's fun, but if I get caught climbing that water tower again . . . or if you go up there and get caught . . . or hurt . . . It would be really bad."

"I don't think I have a choice," Shin said.

"Sure you do."

"No," he said, setting his jaw. "I don't."

With that, he went back inside and closed the door behind him. I thought about following him and arguing some more, but when Shin puts on his stubborn face there's no budging him. If he ever makes up his mind to walk to the moon, I have no doubt he'll get there eventually.

I stop walking and look back at the dome of the tower rising above a horizon of trees. Someone is standing on top of the tower. Two of them. There are two people up there. I can't see what they are doing. Probably workmen replacing the light we broke. Or members of a rival religion, making overtures to the Ten-legged One.

I turn my back on them. I have had enough of towers and gods for one day.

AND THE CORNERS OF THE EARTH WERE DIVIDED, AND THE TWO TRIBES, THE FAITHFUL AND THE PRAGMATISTS, NAMED EACH OTHER EVIL, AND THEY EACH SENT SPIES AND LIES TO PROMOTE RUINATION AND HATRED, AND SO DID THE BITTERNESS SPREAD LIKE BINDWEED ACROSS THE LAND.

23

My father is a lawyer. He thinks he can fix any problem by talking at it.

After he gets home from work, he stops by my room, where I am busy lying flat on my back counting the holes in the acoustic ceiling tiles. He perches one hip on my desk, crosses his arms, and looks me over. Sizing up the opposition.

"Why don't you sit up, Jason. I think we need to talk."

I sit up. I am not looking forward to this.

"I spent a good portion of my afternoon with the city attorney, Jason," he begins. "Your actions last night have caused a lot of problems for a lot of people."

Stage one of the assault is to soften up the enemy with an artillery barrage of guilt.

"I didn't mean to cause anybody any trouble," I say.

"Let me list just a few of the repercussions of your little adventure," he says. "First, there is the matter of the city water supply. Do you realize that they had to drain and sterilize the water tower?"

I shake my head.

"A million gallons of perfectly good water down the drain. Second, there is the time and effort you have cost the city department of public works, the police, fire and rescue . . . not to mention your parents.

"Third, there is the trouble you have caused your friends. And don't try to tell me that little Magda Price would have climbed that tower on her own, or that—"

"Henry would have," I say.

He gives me a long, bland stare, as if he can't quite believe I opened my mouth. After a few long seconds, he continues.

"—or that any of you would have broken into the tank and gone swimming in it—"

It was Henry's idea, I want to say, but I don't.

"—or that any of this would have happened. You have to realize, Jason, that your friends listen to what you say."

They do? I guess they do.

"When you encourage them to do something danger-ous or irresponsible, you are equally—if not more—culpable. If you tell someone to stand in front of a speeding truck, and they do it, you might just as well have killed them with a gun."

The guilt barrage ceases. He inspects me for damage.

Now come the threats.

"You know, of course, that you kids will have to pay for the work the city has to do to clean up the tank and replace the water—more than two thousand dollars."

Two thousand dollars?

"And then there is the damage you have done to yourself, to your reputation, and to your soul."

"My *soul?*"

Again, he gives me that bland stare. Henry's father would have had his belt out.

"Jason, I know all about this little water tower cult you've got going." He shakes his head, calling up his reserves of patience. "I give you credit for being creative. What is it you call yourselves?"

"Chutengodians." I wonder who spilled the secrets of the CTG. Probably Dan. They probably threatened to hit him with a ping-pong ball.

"Chutengodians, yes. Well, that's very clever, but I think your little joke has gone far enough." My father settles into his boring lecture voice. "During their teens, many young people question their religion. They may perceive the church as irrelevant and old-fashioned. They can't see how it has anything to do with their lives. They think that they can worship God on their own terms." *Ladies and gentlemen of the jury, I am old and experienced, while my opponent is young and foolish and irrelevant, which proves my point.*

Anything I could say at this point would get me in trouble. I maintain a neutral silence.

My father mistakes my silence for interest. He goes on: "When I was young I too had my doubts. There were even a few years while I was in college that I hardly went to church at all. I looked at other religions. I even called myself an agnostic for a time." He laughs, shaking his head at the absurdity of it. "But the fact is, Jason, God is real. God is real." *I was once young and foolish too, but now I'm old and foolish, so you should listen to me. I can say anything I want and call it a fact.*

We lock eyes for a few seconds.

"Jason," he says, clasping his hands firmly to demonstrate the unassailability of his argument, "you don't really think that the water tower is God, do you?"

"No."

"Then why would you do that? What on earth were you thinking? Why would you convince your friends to pretend to worship an inanimate object?"

I should really keep silent at this point, but Mr. Mouth has other ideas.

"Why not?" Mr. Mouth says. "What's the difference? None of it's real anyway."

"I'm not joking, Jason."

"Neither am I. Whatever happened to freedom of religion in this country? And what makes you so sure *your* god is the one?"

In a carefully measured voice he says, "Jason, I am not going to engage you in a debate over worshipping a water tower—"

"Forget the water tower. What makes being a

Catholic so special? What about Buddhism, or Hinduism, or whateverism. Look, I admit it was a dumb idea to climb the tower. I'm sorry. But that doesn't make Chutengodianism any dumber than your religion."

He lowers his chin. "You are comparing worshipping a water tower to a two-thousand-year-old religion."

"What's the difference? It's all made up anyway."

I may have gone too far. The vein in his left temple is pulsing.

He stands up abruptly and walks out of the room. Two minutes later he is back, carrying a stack of books.

"Since you're so interested in theology, you might want to read these." He sets the books on my desk. "I'll expect book reports on all five of them a week from next Friday."

Okay, I made a couple of mistakes. Maybe I shouldn't have let Henry open that hatch. Maybe I shouldn't have let Henry into the CTG. Maybe we shouldn't have left the rope ladder hanging from the stairs where the cops could see it. Maybe I shouldn't have climbed the Ten-legged One. I don't know. But I don't see where it's going to do anyone any good for me to get eyestrain from reading a bunch of Catholic propaganda, and not get my driver's license, and spend hours shut in my room, and whatever else they've got cooked up. It's persecution is what it is. Religious intolerance. A violation of the separation of church and Jason. A trampling of my individual rights.

What would Jesus do? I ask myself. What would Martin Luther do? What would Muhammad do? What would Moses do? They would cry out, "Let my people go!"

I will gather the Chutengodians, and together we will set off across the freeways and farms. I will part the rivers with my staff. We will cross deserts, and scale mountains and we will come to a new land, a new Eden, where water towers dot the landscape, protecting us with the power of their great wet heads.

I look out the window at the dome of the Ten-legged One, and suddenly I am back inside, swimming in darkness, holding tight to Magda's hand.

Me: Why is it that new religions always get persecuted?

Just Al: What do you mean?

Me: The Jews were persecuted by the Egyptians, the Christians were persecuted by the Romans, and the Protestants were persecuted by the Catholics. The Pilgrims came to America because everybody in England was giving them a hard time. Every time somebody starts up a new religion, the old religions get all twisted over it.

Just Al: I, uh, er . . .

Me: What does the pope care if some kid in St. Andrew Valley decides to worship dogs?

Just Al: Ha ha ha!

Brianna: Jason, you are so lame!

I catch Magda's eye and wink at her, Chutengodian to Chutengodian. She looks away, flustered.

Me: This is a democracy, right? I mean, I have a right to worship dog piss if I want to.
Brianna: That is just sick.
George: Why dog piss?
Me: Why anything? Why not worship the sun? Why not worship a water tower? Isn't it arbitrary?
Tracy: How can it be arbitrary? God isn't a made-up *thing*. He's *God*.
Me: Prove it.
Tracy: I don't have to *prove* it. I *know* it.
Just Al: I have to agree with Tracy here. I *know* that God is real. I feel his presence in my heart.
Me: What does it feel like?
Just Al: It's hard to describe, Jason. It feels good.
Me: Oh. I thought maybe it was like heartburn or something.

The TPO meeting ends with one of Just Al's ridiculous prayers, something about Jesus being "one cool dude." On the way out I catch Magda in the hallway.

"Hey, how are you doing?" I ask.

"In trouble up to my ears."

"Me too. I'm a prisoner. And my dad is making me read a bunch of books."

"That's not so bad. You like to read."

"You haven't seen the books. Plus, he wants me to write book reports on them."

"Oh. Well, I've pulled permanent baby-sitting duty for my little brothers. They even made me quit my job at Wigglesworth's. I'm surprised my parents even let me out of the house for TPO. They think you guys corrupted me."

"Did we?"

She grins. "Maybe just a little. Have you talked to Henry?"

"Yeah. He's already planning another swimming party."

Magda laughs, and I feel it inside my chest.

There is nothing in the world I would rather do than make Magda Price laugh.

"He's funny," she says.

"Who, Henry? I thought you thought he was scary."

"Scary on the outside, sure. But he's got a good heart."

I think, *Good heart?* What does *that* mean? Don't *I* have a good heart?

I say, "Oh."

24

For the next several days I stay close to home, playing the part of a penitent sinner. I am Cain, I am Judas. But inside, I am Paul the Apostle, I am Nelson Mandela, I am the Bird Man of Alcatraz. They can imprison me, they can bury me in religious tracts, they can take away my Xbox—but they can never destroy the spirit of Chutengodianism.

Secretly, in the dead of night, I begin work on a comic book based upon the Chutengodian Midnight Mass. Only difference is, I add a scene where the Chutengodian Commandments appear etched upon the steel walls of the tank:

I. Thou shalt not be a jerk.

II. Get a life.

III. Thou shalt not eat asparagus.

The third one is kind of personal, I admit. I've never liked asparagus. But the first two offer good, solid advice for anybody, and they aren't really covered in the original ten. I move on to the baptism scene.

I'm not the best artist in the world, but I'm not bad. Usually you can tell what it is I'm trying to draw, but I'm having trouble with the scenes inside the Godhead. I can't seem to capture that vast, echoey space. After a while I give up on the background and just work on Magda swimming in her bra and panties.

Maybe I'll give it to her for a present.

Someday.

I tried to read some of the books my dad gave me. I got about ten pages into *Why I am a Catholic* before accidentally-on-purpose dropping it in the bathtub. Ooops. It is drying now. Amazing how thick a book gets when it's been drenched and dried.

Teen Spirit: The Holy Trinity for Today's Youth, was not much better. I gave up on that one halfway through the table of contents. I looked at *Teen Jesus: His Life and Times* for about thirty seconds. I'd rather read a user's guide for a Korean DVD player—at least that's good for some humor. As for the other two books, I haven't exactly opened them.

I've got less than two weeks to turn in my book reports. Maybe World War III will break out, or a rogue comet will destroy North America, or something else will come along to save me.

By Tuesday I'm pretty much stir crazy, so as soon as my mother leaves for her bridge club, I take off to see how Shin is doing. I knock on his window. No answer. Then I hear Shin's voice, chanting softly.

". . . and first there was the Ocean and the Ocean was alone, and first there was the Ocean and the . . ."

I look around. No Shin, but I can still hear the voice. I back up a few steps. There he is, standing on the peak of the roof staring down at the ground. His face is pale and shiny with sweat.

"Shin!" I shout.

He jerks like he's been jabbed with a needle.

"What are you doing?" I ask.

He looks down at me. "Practicing."

I notice that he has a rope tied around his waist.

"Practicing what?"

"Being scared."

"What's the rope for?"

"I've got the other end tied to the chimney. Just in case."

"How'd you get up there?"

He points. At the corner of the house I see a bright yellow fiberglass ladder leaning against the eaves.

"Why do you want to be scared?" I ask, more curious than worried now.

"I'm going up." His pointing finger swings toward the tower.

"I don't know if you should . . ."

"I *have* to go up."

"There's nothing up there."

"That's not what you said last week. You *swam* in him."

"Yeah, and Henry almost got killed, Magda and I are under house arrest, and I think Dan is being tortured in a dungeon someplace. It's not worth it."

Shin shakes his head. "You don't understand. I *have* to go."

"Maybe you're taking this thing a little too seriously."

"Maybe *you're* not serious enough." He glares at me, his lip quivering. "He talks to me, you know. I hear what he says." He looks toward the tower.

"Shin, you're scaring me."

His face reddens. "You think I care if you're scared?" he shouts. "He doesn't want *you*, he wants *me*!" He is balanced on the edge of the roof, his fear of heights obliterated by anger.

"Be careful!" I say.

"*You* think it's a joke. *You* let Henry Stagg spoil everything. *You* left me on the steps. *You* left *me*." His cheeks are wet.

"Shin, come on down."

"Screw you," he sobs.

I hear a car pull into the driveway. Mrs. Schinner jumps out, gray-streaked red hair flying around her head. "Peter!" she screams.

Shin steps back from the edge and shrinks about a third.

"Peter!" she shrieks again. "What are you *doing*?"

"It's okay, Mrs. Schinner," I say. "He's got a rope tied to him."

She whirls on me. "You! What are you doing here?"

"Nothing! I just—"

She is looking up again. "Peter! You get down from there right now!"

Shin, his hands shaking, is untying the rope. Mrs. Schinner turns back to me, hair whipping across her face.

"You put him up to this, Jason."

"He was up there when I got here!"

"You—" She stabs the air between us with a long forefinger. "—are a bad influence." I take a step back. Her eyes are quivering, her lips tight and hard. "Leave here this instant."

Shin is clutching the end of his rope, watching us with an expression I can only describe as shattered.

"You need help getting down?" I ask him.

He shakes his head.

"Leave!" says Mrs. Schinner.

I leave.

What would have happened if Shin had fallen while I was standing there? What if he had hurt himself, or died? Would Mrs. Schinner want me sent to jail for murder? How could she hold me responsible for Shin's behavior? I didn't *do* anything.

"Yes, your honor, I pulled up in my car and there he

was, the Kahuna, encouraging my son to leap from the roof to his death."

"Objection! The witness could not have heard anything my client said from inside her car!"

"Objection overruled. The defendant's mere presence at the scene proves his guilt. Bailiff! Escort this lying, murderous scumbag to the rat-infested dungeons."

I suppose that Mrs. Schinner will say something to my parents, and I'll be busted for violating the terms of my incarceration. Oh well, nothing I can do about that now. I start for home, then I remember that Henry Stagg was supposed to get out of the hospital the day before yesterday.

ᴀɴᴅ ᴛʜᴇ ᴄʟᴏᴜᴅs ᴏꜰ ᴡᴀʀ ᴅɪᴅ ᴅᴇsᴄᴇɴᴅ ᴜᴘᴏɴ
ᴛʜᴇ Eᴀʀᴛʜ, ᴀɴᴅ ᴛʜᴇ ɢʀᴇᴀᴛ ᴀʀᴍɪᴇs ᴄᴀᴍᴇ
ᴛᴏɢᴇᴛʜᴇʀ ɪɴ ᴀ ʜᴏʟᴏᴄᴀᴜsᴛ ᴏꜰ ꜰɪʀᴇ ᴀɴᴅ ᴡɪɴᴅ, ᴀɴᴅ
ᴛʜᴇʏ ꜰᴏᴜɢʜᴛ ꜰʀᴏᴍ ᴅᴀᴡɴ ᴛᴏ ᴅᴜsᴋ, ᴀɴᴅ ᴛʜᴇ
Pʀᴀɢᴍᴀᴛɪsᴛs ᴘʀᴇᴠᴀɪʟᴇᴅ ᴏɴ ᴛʜᴇ ꜰɪʀsᴛ ᴅᴀʏ ᴏꜰ ᴛʜᴇ
Gʀᴇᴀᴛ Wᴀʀ.

25

Janice, Henry's older sister, answers
the door. She looks just like Henry, only with longer
hair, and breasts.

"Well, if it isn't a member of the St. Andrew Valley
Synchronized Water Tower Swim Team," she says. "I
suppose you're looking for my idiot brother."

"Is he home?"

"Yeah, and he's not going anywhere for a while.
C'mon in."

I go back to Henry's room and find him in his bed
reading the latest issue of *Analog*. He looks at me and
grins.

"Kahuna! How's it going?"

"Okay. How are you?"

"How do I look?" His right leg is held rigid from his

hip to his foot by a plastic and foam splint. It is open at the end, revealing five grayish toes.

"Not great," I say.

"I know. This sucks. Hey, you want to sign my splint?"

"Why?"

"I don't know. Isn't that what you're supposed to do?"

"Okay." I take the pen he offers me. The plastic splint already has several signatures scrawled on it, including Mitch, Marsh, and Bobby—the three stooges. And one that says, *Get well soon! XXXOOO, Magda.*

"Magda was here?"

"She brought me a box of chocolates and helped me eat them."

"Oh." I draw a picture of a figure wearing cowboy boots falling off a water tower. In my picture, he misses the catwalk.

Henry looks at it and frowns. "You know something? I never got my boots back."

"You won't be wearing them for a while anyway."

"True. Hey, I thought you were permanently grounded."

"I'm AWOL. I was just over at Shin's. He was up on his roof working on his fear of heights. He still wants to go up."

Henry laughs, and I feel guilty for sharing this with him. Shin would hate me.

Henry says, "There is *no way* Schinner is going up that tower, I don't care how many rope ladders you build for him."

"You don't know Shin," I say.

"Why would I want to?"

"Well, for one thing, he's smarter than you and me put together."

Henry rolls his eyes. "So's a computer. That doesn't mean it can climb."

"You don't know him," I say again. "He's stubborn as a cat."

Henry looks past me and grins. "Hey! Mitch, my man! Burgers and fries, what a guy!"

Mitch Cosmo is standing in the bedroom doorway holding two large paper McDonalds sacks. Bobby Whatever and Marsh Andrews are crowding through the door behind him.

"I hope you guys brought enough for his Kahunaness," Henry says.

Mitch looks doubtful. The smell of burgers and fries rolls into the room.

"That's okay," I say. "I'm not hungry."

"You sure?" Henry says. "It's in the commandments, right? Treat your fellow Choots right."

"What's a choot?" I ask.

"We're Choots," says Marsh.

"What commandments?" I ask.

"Show him, Mitch."

Mitch sets the McDonalds bags down, reaches into his pocket, and comes out with a grimy, folded sheet of paper. He unfolds the paper, looks it over like a chimpanzee studying a menu, and hands it to me.

The Chootengodiun Commanments

For a moment I am speechless. Not only has Henry come up with his own set of commandments, he has invited his stooges into the CTG.

"You spelled Chutengodian wrong," I say.

Henry laughs, echoed by the stooges.

"You spelled 'Commandments' wrong, too," I say.

"At least we're consistent," Henry says, opening one of the McDonalds bags.

I read down the list of "commanments."

1. Don't be a wuss
2. Don't forget to duck
3. Don't take any shit
4. Honor your fellow Choots
5. Don't fall
6. Don't get caught

"You couldn't come up with ten?" I say, ignoring the fact that I came up with only three.

"We're working on it," Henry says, unwrapping a cheeseburger. The stooges are also digging in; the sound of crinkling paper is deafening, and my mouth is watering. "You want some fries?"

"No. Listen, you can't just make up your own rules."

"Why not?"

"Because I already *have* the Chutengodian Commandments."

"So now we got six more. Besides, I didn't make them up by myself."

"You had help from *these* guys?" I say with a sneer.

"Me and the High Priestess came up with them. Mitch just wrote 'em down."

"Magda?"

"Yup."

I rip the sheet of paper in half and let the torn paper flutter to the floor. "Your commandments are null and void."

Henry laughs. "You can't do that. I'm the High Priest."

"Well I'm the Founder and Head Kahuna."

"I still don't know what a Kahuna is."

"Like I told you, I'm your pope."

"Not my pope. We Choots are Protestants." He shoves a fry in his mouth. "Protestant Choots don't recognize the pope. It's the Choots versus the Chutengodians. And by the way, the tower is off limits to you."

"We go where we want," I say.

"Who? You and Shin? Gimme a break."

"Me and Shin and Magda and Dan."

"I don't care about Danny. As for Magda, she's with us, your Kahunaness."

"We'll see about that," I say, shoving my way past the Protestant stooges and out the door.

"Thanks for stopping by!" Henry calls after me.

I get home about five minutes before my mother returns from her bridge club. I am congratulating myself for my excellent timing when the phone rings. A few minutes later my mother opens my bedroom door and crosses her arms and gives me a look that I do not like one bit.

"That was Mrs. Schinner," she says.

Busted.

She is giving me that intense look she gets when she suspects me of having a new disease. "Jason, whatever were you thinking?"

"Sorry," I say. "I just needed to get out."

"That poor boy could have fallen and hurt himself."

"He had a rope tied to his waist. He would've just sort of hung there."

"Jason!"

"Look, I just went over there to see how he was doing. He was already on the roof when I got there."

"Jason, I don't even want to hear it," she says, holding up her palms.

"I'm *sorry.*"

She flaps her hands, beating away my words, then turns and slams the door behind her.

My mother, slamming the door. That's different.

So the Faithful gathered in the forests and on the mountains and in dark caverns, and they prepared themselves, and on the night of the second day they immersed themselves in the rivers and streams. And others of them waded out into the lakes and the seas, or marched upon the glaciers. And at dawn on the third day, they called upon the Ocean's Avatars to strike.

26

Being pope sucks. I guess that's why they hire those old guys to do the job. Maybe at their age they just don't care. I try not to care, but it's hard. I'm stuck here with no phone, no Xbox, nothing to do but read and draw pictures. I pick up the *Teen Jesus* book and flip through it. Did Jesus have problems like this? I guess so. They ended up nailing him to a cross.

I toss the book back on the floor.

What if Shin and I hadn't run into Henry that day? What if Henry hadn't slugged me, and I hadn't looked up at the belly of the tower all woozy and stunned? Chutengodianism might never have happened. We would never have climbed that tower, or swum in the Godhead. Henry would not be lying broken in bed. Shin would be collecting pods instead of climbing on his roof.

And me, I'd be doing whatever I wanted to do.

I wonder what that would be. Maybe I'd be doing something with Magda. Has she really become a "Choot"? I just can't see her hanging out with Henry and his stooges, but you never know what a girl will do. I open my sketchbook and look at the drawing I made of her swimming in the tank, her mouth open, gulping air, her smooth legs kicking up bubbles, her breasts pushing out against her wet bra. I think I made her arms a little too short, but she's still beautiful.

Maybe Magda and I could start over like Adam and Eve. Convert some new members. Not violent juvenile delinquents like Henry, but normal, healthy, sane types. Like Dan, only not Dan. We could convert them one at a time. Me and Magda, Head Kahuna and High Priestess. Let Henry have his little sect.

As for Shin, he's gone off in his own direction. I wish I could call him. If I could get him talking about pods and video games I think he'd be okay. The thing about Shin that nobody else understands is that he has a high-speed, one-track, damn-the-torpedoes-full-speed-ahead mind. When he gets going on something he just *goes*. When it's something like snails it's pretty harmless, but now that he's fixated on water towers and Chutengodianism . . . I don't know.

Maybe I never should have brought it up with him. Shin was happier when he was his own god—the Pod God. Now his snails are all estivating. He's not a god any-more, he's just a cult of one, listening to voices in his head.

Something my father said comes back to me: *You have to realize, Jason, that your friends listen to what you say.*

Maybe Mrs. Schinner was right. Maybe I am a bad influence.

I turn to a fresh page in my sketchbook. I hold my pencil poised over the white expanse, but my mind is as blank as the paper. The Founder and Head Kahuna of the Church of the Ten-legged God has run out of ideas.

For the next two days things are very tense at Bock Penitentiary. The prisoner, sentenced to solitary confinement, is surly and unrepentant. The guards are suspicious and quick to mete out punishment.

On Thursday they force the prisoner to accept correctional therapy. He is delivered from Bock Penitentiary to the Church of the Good Shepherd Brainwashing Facility by armored vehicle. The transport route takes them past the St. Andrew Valley water tower. The prisoner looks up at the great bulging tank and notices graffiti spray-painted in bright red on its side. He looks closer and sees that the marks are words. He reads:

DON'T BE A WUSS

"Uh-oh," says the prisoner.

"What's that?" asks the male guard. "Did you say something, Jason?"

"No," I say. "It's nothing."

Just Al: Jason? You haven't had much to say this evening.

Me: Sorry. What are we talking about?

Just Al: We were discussing the church's position on abortion.

Me: What about it?

Brianna: There's a Life Teen rally in Fairview next Saturday. A bunch of us are going.

Just Al: We've arranged to use three school buses, so there's plenty of room for everybody.

Me: Sorry, not interested.

Brianna: You wouldn't be, Jason. You probably think all babies should be killed.

Me: I can think of at least one who wouldn't have been missed.

Just Al: Come on now. Let's keep things civil.

Brianna: He thinks he can say anything he wants.

Me: It's called freedom of speech.

Just Al: Speaking of freedom of speech, let's talk a bit about the vandalism that occurred last night. I'm talking about the graffiti on the water tower.

Brianna: I think it's totally stupid.

Tracy: I heard it was a cult.

Magda: It's not a cult. Just some kids messing around.

Tracy: How do *you* know?

Magda: I just do.

Just Al: The question is, why isn't spray-painting a message on public property protected by free speech?

Brianna: Because it's *public* property.

Just Al: But we can have a pro-life rally on public property, and that *is* protected. How are the two things different?

Me: One is a waste of paint; the other is a waste of time.

Brianna: Jason, you are so lame.

I look over at Magda, but she won't meet my eyes. The meeting goes on. I have nothing more to say on any subject. Why should I get myself in more trouble? Ten hours later (or so it seems), Just Al finally releases us.

"Hey, Magda," I say as we push our chairs back to the side of the room. "I've got to talk to you."

"I have to go, Jason. My mom's outside waiting for me."

"Can't you get out sometime? How about we meet at Wigglesworth's?"

"Jason, I can't. I'll get in trouble."

"You got out to see Henry."

"That was different. He was hurt."

"He said you've become a Choot."

"A what?"

"A Protestant."

"Look, Jason, I don't know what you're talking about, and I don't care. I don't care about your water tower, or being High Priestess, or any of that. Things at home aren't so good right now. I can't afford to mess up."

"How about if I come over to your house then?"

"Somebody would see you."

"I'll call you then, sometime when your parents aren't home."

"I'm not allowed to talk on the phone."

"So what? Neither am I!"

She gives me a pained look. "Jason, I'm sorry. I just can't."

"How about—"

"I have to go," she says, and she does.

And as the sun rose and touched the heads of the towering Avatars, the Pragmatists did look up in fear and awe, and a great cry of holy terror arose, and was heard in every land.

27

The next morning, with my father at work and my mother off shopping, I make the mistake of answering the doorbell. The Gestapo are on the front steps, scouring the neighborhood for Chutengodians. Officer Gerry Kramer and his Gestapo sidekick (Officer Firfth, according to the brass plate above his badge) give me that bland I-know-you're-lying-you-Chutengodian-scum look.

"Good morning, Jason," Kramer says. "We'd like to ask you a few questions."

"I'm not supposed to have guests." *Bock, Jason Bock. Prisoner number 7238659.*

"I'm not surprised," Kramer says with a near-smile. "That was some stunt you pulled last week."

I shrug, admitting to nothing. *I may be doomt, bot zee reseeztance weel live on!*

"I suppose you've noticed the graffiti on the tower?"

"I saw it." *Oui.*

"Did you put it there?"

"No." *Non.*

Firfth says, "We know all about your little water tower cult." *Chutengodian scum!*

"It's not a cult," I say. "And it wasn't me who painted the tower. I just noticed it yesterday." *I am eenocent!*

"Do you know what it's going to cost the city to get up there and clean it up?" Firfth says, getting a little pink around the eyes.

I resort to silence, terrified that I will be called upon to pronounce the name "Firfth."

Gerry Kramer says, "Jason, you and Henry and Dan Grant and Magda Price were caught up there two weeks ago. And we know that Peter Schinner is a member of your little . . . organization. Two nights ago, one of you was up there with a can of spray paint. We know it wasn't Henry." His eyes drill into me.

Your theenkeen eez flawed, mon Capitan. Eet wuz not I who destroyed zee bridge, and eefen eef I knew who zee geelty party wuz, you woood not lairn eet from me! Of course, I know it was Henry's stooges—the Choots—who spray-painted the Ten-legged One. But I'm not going to rat them out.

"Maybe it was some kids from Fairview," I suggest.

Gerry Kramer shakes his head, smiling but unamused.

"Jason, you must know we'll find out who did it sooner or later. Do yourself a favor."

"Look, I didn't do it, okay? Last time I was up there I nearly drowned, and Henry got all busted up, and they're making us pay for replacing all the water, and I'm grounded for the rest of my natural life. Believe me, the view wasn't worth it. I'm not the mad graffiti climber you take me for."

Kramer's expression changes somewhat. He almost believes me.

I say, "I'm telling you the truth. I've climbed my last water tower."

Maybe my mother is right. Maybe I really do have sleeping sickness. After the Gestapo leave I lie down and sleep the rest of the day away, waking up every now and then to stare at the ceiling. There are eighty-six holes in each ceiling tile.

Shortly before dinner, I pick up *The Seven Storey Mountain,* one of the books my father dumped on me. It's a particularly thick one. I skip over the preface and the introduction and am able to read about ten pages before my brain starts sputtering. I skip to the end of the book to see how it turns out, but it's more of the same. To prevent brain meltdown, I slam the book shut. How am I supposed to write a report about an unreadable book? What is there to say?

After dinner I sit down and attempt to write a book report on the book I have just not read.

Book Report

The Seven Storey Mountain

This is a book by a man named Thomas Merton about himself. The book, when you start reading it, is likely to cause a cerebral event of a painful nature due to its complicated use of the English language and subject matter. There may be a mountain in it, and the mountain may have seven stories, but I couldn't swear to it. In the end, nothing much has changed really except for the fact that he is still a Catholic and you are done reading. I would recommend this book to anyone because it feels so good to be done with it.

I do not think my father will be amused. I crumple the page and file it under Trash.

I take one more stab at my reading assignment—this time I read more about *Teen Jesus: His Life and Times*. I actually get about twenty pages into it before the brain freeze hits.

I have nothing in common with this kid. I'm not interested in woodworking, I don't have a beard, and my mom's not a virgin, as far as I know.

I set the book aside and devote the next few hours to feeling sorry for myself. This has not been my greatest summer ever. I founded a religion, sure, but look what's come of it. Henry Stagg has perverted Chutengodianism to his own dark purposes. Dan has disappeared like the frightened, backstabbing rat he is. Magda won't talk to me. Shin has spun off into some strange Shinnish reality.

And me, I'm sitting in my room surrounded by unreadable propaganda and bored out of my skull.

Time . . .

I count the holes in yet another ceiling tile. I come up with eighty-six, again! Apparently, all the ceiling tiles have exactly the same number of holes. Remarkable. Maybe there is a god after all!

. . . passes . . .

I close my eyes and watch the patterns that appear on the back of my eyelids. A honeycomb pattern morphs into a pulsing, jumping asterisk. Am I seeing the structure of the universe, or the random firing of synapses?

. . . slowly . . .

At 1:13 A.M., still wide-awake, still bored, I am staring out the window through the rain at the red light atop the Ten-legged One. Every time it blinks my thoughts shift.

Flash.

Thunder in the distance. We're going to have a storm.

Flash.

The whole thing started with Henry.

Flash.

But I didn't have to get Shin involved.

Flash.

Magda went to see Henry but she won't see me.

Flash.

I hope Shin is okay. I should've known he'd take it too far.

Flash.

It's all my fault. Bringing Chutengodianism to Shin was like giving a can of gasoline to a pyromaniac.

Flash.

Henry is like Martin Luther, breaking away from Rome.

Flash.

Magda hates me.

Flash.

I should go off into the desert for forty days. Isn't that what Jesus did? Or was that Moses? I'll pack a bag and leave St. Andrew Valley for a few months. Become a religious exile. Get a job. See if anybody misses me. I have about two hundred dollars stashed away. That should be enough. Maybe I'll start a new church in another town with another water tower—the Eight-legged, or the Five-legged One. I'll start small—just one or two acolytes. We'll hold services under the tower, not on top of it. We'll . . .

Where's the light? I look hard out the window, but I see no flashing light . . .

Flash.

There it is. I wonder where it—

Flash.

—went. Maybe a momentary electrical failure or something. What was I thinking about? Oh yeah, going off to start a new . . . *where's the light?*

. . .

I see a half flash, then the light is gone.

. . .

Then it returns.

Flash.

Somebody is up there. On the tower. Moving around. Blocking the light.

Flash.

Probably one of Henry's stooges, doing something I'll be blamed for. Some blasphemous, destructive act. Spray-painting more "commanments" probably. But if they're writing more graffiti, why are they blocking the light on the very top of the tank?

I see a flicker on the horizon; a few seconds later I hear thunder. The storm is getting closer.

Maybe it's terrorists sabotaging the water. Adding anthrax, or arsenic, or something. For the briefest instant I consider calling the cops. I know that's what I *should* do, but I also know that I won't. Whoever's on the water tower might just be there for the view. Except that they had better not stay there much longer, not with a storm on the way. The tower is the tallest structure for many miles, a lightning magnet.

Flash.

Standing up there during a thunderstorm would be suicidal. Even the stooges couldn't be that stupid.

Flash.

If it's the stooges.

Flash.

Who else could it be?

Flash.

I do not like what I am thinking.

. . .

The light disappears again.

. . .

I tie on my black Reeboks.

. . .

I don't want to risk sneaking past my parents' bedroom, so I climb out my window. It's not raining yet, but the air feels thick. The rumble of thunder is constant from the west. I run, ninja feet whispering on tarmac.

A ND LO, THE AVATARS DID MARCH UPON THE PRAGMATISTS, AND FROM THE SKY CAME A DELUGE SUCH AS EARTH HAD NEVER KNOWN, AND THE PRAGMATISTS WERE SWEPT AWAY ON A GREAT TIDE, AND THE LANDS OF EARTH SANK BENEATH THE WAVES.

28

By the time I reach the tower the air is still and thick, the way it gets before a big storm. Every few seconds the western horizon is lit up by lightning flashes. I look up at the belly of the tank. Is he still up there?

There is something leaning against the central column, what I least want to see: a yellow fiberglass extension ladder. The same ladder I saw three days ago leaning against the eaves of Shin's house.

He did it. Shin climbed the Ten-legged One. I am both angry and proud.

The tower is lit by a bright flash. Seconds later the *badda-dooom* of not-so-distant thunder rolls in. The wind is picking up; I can hear the rustle of leaves in the trees. I cup my hands around my mouth and shout.

"Shiiiiin!"

My voice is snatched and disintegrated by the wind. Another lightning flash lights up the legs of the tower, crisp and bright, leaving stripy afterimages on my retinas. I count five seconds to the next *badda-dooom.* Very close now—only about a mile away. I follow the spiral staircase up the column with my eyes, along the first catwalk, up the ladder to the upper catwalk. No Shin in sight.

He's not coming down. Either he froze up again or he's trying to kill himself. Or maybe he thinks the Ten-legged One will protect him. I have no such illusions. The thought of climbing back up those metal stairs during an electrical storm scares the crap out of me. I should call the cops. But it would take them twenty minutes or more to respond, and the storm will be here in full force, and then what would they do?

Nothing.

A large raindrop splashes my shoulder, then another.

I start climbing.

The wind is coming harder now, bringing with it rain. I climb quickly, my hands sliding along the metal railings, trying to remember everything I know about lightning. If the tower gets hit now, how dead am I? How often is the tower struck? Does it happen with every storm? I don't know these things, but I do know that this is a very bad place to be right now. By the time I reach the lower catwalk the rain is coming down in sheets. For the moment I am protected beneath the tank, but now I have to follow the catwalk out from the central column to the legs, then up the ladder to the upper catwalk, where I'll be completely exposed. I pause for a few seconds to catch my breath.

An intense flash blinds me, followed instantly by an eardrum-ripping thunderclap. I fall to my knees, my eyes crazed with afterimages. Did it hit the tower? No, but it was close. I blink a few times, feeling my heart jumping in my chest like an insane frog.

"Keep moving," I say to myself. I follow the catwalk to the ladder. By the time I reach the upper catwalk I am completely drenched. I keep moving around the perimeter, past the spray-painted, four-foot-high letters:

DON'T BE A WUSS

The wind is whipping around the tank; raindrops hitting from every direction. I reach the ladder leading to the top of the tower. *Don't be a wuss.* I climb up and over the dome of the tower. I see a thin, dark figure standing with his arms wrapped around the blinking red aviation light.

"Shin!" I yell.

He doesn't move. His head is tipped back. He is staring straight up into the rain. Sodden X-Men pajamas cling to his scrawny limbs like fur to a wet cat. I grab him by the shoulder and shake.

"Shin! Are you okay?"

His head tips toward me; his eyes flutter open. I don't think he recognizes me.

"Shin! We have to get down!"

He sees me now. "Jay?"

"Yes. Come on. You climbed up here; you can climb down." I try to pry his hands loose from the light housing. It's like trying to untie a wet knot.

"We have to go inside," he says.

"We have to go *down*."

"Yes. Down." He points at the hatch. Lightning flashes and my retinas are branded by the image of a new padlock. And a hacksaw. Shin has been trying to cut through the lock.

Thunder slams my ears. Too close. My ears are ringing. I smell ozone.

"Shin, we're gonna get fried up here."

"That's why we have to get inside."

"Are you crazy?"

"We'll be safe in the water."

"No! Damn it, Shin, we have to go down."

"It'll open for you. You're the Kahuna."

"No! We gotta get down, Shin."

"I can't."

"Yes, you can."

"The water is safe."

Another lightning flash, and I see his face clearly: pale, goggle-eyed, and frightened—but strangely calm and sane. He says, "We'll be safe in the water. If lightning strikes the tank the current will travel along the metal superstructure."

"Are you sure?"

He nods. I believe him. Shin is a crazy gastropod god, a social disaster, and now a religious maniac—but he knows his science. If he says we'll be safe in the water, I believe him.

"When we get out of this," I say, "I am going to pound you." I mean it. I'm that mad at him. I grab the hacksaw and saw furiously at the lock, certain that we are about to be incinerated by the next lightning bolt, converted to two huge, four-limbed lumps of charcoal. I wonder if we'll shatter when we hit the ground.

Shin watches, hugging the light. It takes about a hundred of those red flashes before the saw cuts through the lock. I swing the hatch up.

Shin unravels himself from the post and peers into the opening.

"It's dark," he says.

"There's a platform a few feet down," I say. "I'll go first."

I grab the edge, and lower myself down through the hole to the platform. It's a relief to be out of the rain.

"Okay," I shout. Shin's feet appear. I grab his ankles and help him down. Standing face-to-face on the tiny platform, I can barely make out the shape of his head.

"I can't see," he says.

"What did you expect?"

"I don't know."

"You said we have to be in the water to be safe, right?"

"I think so."

The sky lights up with a thunderclap that is so loud and close I can feel it vibrate the shell of the tank.

I say, "Maybe this is a stupid question, but you know how to swim, right?"

"Of course I do," Shin says.

"Good."

I shove him off the platform.

AND ALL THE FOUR-LEGGED CREATURES OF THE EARTH DID DROWN. AND THE REPTILES THAT CRAWLED UPON THEIR BELLIES DID DROWN AS WELL. AND THOSE WHO WALKED UPON TWO LEGS, THEY DROWNED TOO, WITH NEITHER PRAGMATIST NOR FAITHFUL SPARED FROM THE FURY OF THE OCEAN.

29

It took three hours for the storm to pass. Shin and I spent most of the time hanging on to the bottom of the ladder, talking. Actually, Shin did most of the talking. I just listened. Listened as my best friend told me the "truth" about water towers. I had not realized, you see, that the ocean was a conscious entity, or that the towers could walk.

"In fact," Shin said, "when we climb out of here, we could be miles from St. Andrew Valley. The gods frequently shift location at night, moving from town to town."

"Gods?"

"Demigods, actually. The towers are Avatars of the Ocean, subject to his might. They move at night."

"I wonder why I never noticed that," I said.

"Because the Ocean did not wish you to notice."

"Oh."

"In fact, I'm pretty sure that they transition by employing a form of antigravitronic pulse. That would also explain how they are able to move through inter-stellar space. See, the Ocean originally came from another part of the galaxy by means of the towers. Hundreds of millions of them landed here, injected their water cargo into the Earth, then self-destructed. That's why iron is the fourth most common element on earth. And so much water. Of course, that all happened a couple billion years ago."

"I thought people built the towers."

"That's what they want you to think."

"You're serious," I said.

"I know it sounds unbelievable," Shin said in a voice that sounded completely sane, "but it's true. I've been talking to them. It's quite a burden, you know, being chosen. You must know. You've been chosen too."

"I have?"

"You are the one. You opened my eyes and ears."

"I didn't mean to."

"At first I doubted what they were telling me, but the signs are clear."

A white flash from above, beaming through the hatch and lighting up the interior for an instant just as the walls of the tank rang like an enormous gong, shivering the surface of the water.

"You see?" he said. "We are under the protection of the Ten-legged One."

"Did we just get struck by lightning?"

"Yes. It is a sign."

When the sounds of the storm finally faded, I suggested it was time to climb out of the tank, but Shin refused to budge.

"I'm staying," he said.

I couldn't talk him up the ladder. I don't think he was afraid, he just didn't want to leave.

"I feel safe here," he said.

So I climbed out of the tank and down the tower and walked to the Amoco station and called the cops on my best friend. I waited and watched as the police and the fire department spent the rest of the night trying to figure out how the coax the Chosen One out of that tank.

It was light out when they finally dragged him, kicking and shouting, out into the morning sun.

30

I am searching for beer bottles, crumpled newspapers, car parts, fast food wrappers, soda cans, and other fascinating items. When I find one of these treasures, I stab it with my litter poker and scrape it off into a blue plastic bag. Here on the grassy shoulders of Route 17, the hunting is good. My first bag is almost full, and I have only been searching for an hour.

Seven hours to go.

I am wearing a fluorescent orange vest. I can see another orange vest a few hundred yards away on the other side of the highway. The shoulders of Route 17 are dotted with garbage-pickers. Some of them are volunteers, doing their part to make St. Andrew Valley a cleaner, prettier place to live. Me? I'm paying my debt to society, which has been calculated at 210 hours of community service.

Only 209 hours to go.

I'm bored.

For a while I keep myself going by fantasizing. I imagine myself coming across a hundred-dollar bill. A gold ring. A bagful of hundred-dollar bills. A mint copy of *X-Men* number one.

Instead, I find a soggy grocery bag, a cigar butt, an armless plastic doll, a broken hubcap, and the dried-up corpse of a muskrat. I leave the muskrat behind.

I've almost caught up with the guy ahead of me. He must be picking up every cigarette butt and bottlecap. I wonder who he is, and what sort of civic guilt caused him to sign up for garbage duty. I watch him stop, jab a tiny scrap of paper with his poker, and carefully transfer it to his blue bag. His movements are so slow and deliberate I want to run across the highway and grab him and shake him.

That's when I recognize Dan Grant. I haven't seen Dan since the night Henry fell off the water tower. I didn't realize he was on the clean-up crew. He must have been dropped off by a different van.

He stops, bends over, picks up a brown bottle, pours a few ounces of stale beer, and drops it into his bag. He looks just as bored as I feel.

As his spiritual leader, I feel an obligation to make his life a little more interesting. I drop my bag and run back to the muskrat. It's still dead. I impale the flattened beast on my poker and carry it across the highway. Dan, intent on a scrap of newspaper, does not see me sneaking up behind him with my muskrat-on-a-stick. When I'm a few feet away I fling the muskrat over his head. It lands right at his feet.

Dan lets out a yelp and jumps straight up, almost as if the soles of his shoes have exploded. He lands and leaps again, this time straight back into me. We both fall down. I'm laughing.

"Greetings from the Ten-legged One," I say.

He rolls away from me and scrambles to his feet.

"Jason?"

"You shoulda seen yourself jump," I say.

He looks from me to the muskrat. "That's not funny," he says.

"Sure it is."

"You've got a warped sense of humor."

"I know. So how you been?" I ask.

"Better, since I quit hanging out with you."

"What did I do?"

"What *didn't* you do? Look at us. Picking up cigarette butts eight hours a day."

"You think that's my fault?"

"Look what happened to Henry and Shin. Henry's all busted up. They got Magda working at the homeless shelter washing dishes. And Shin has gone insane."

"He's not insane."

"What do you call it when they lock you in the psych ward?"

"That was just for a couple days. He's home now. He's fine."

"You've seen him?"

"No, but I called him." It's true. I called him. But his mother picked up the phone and told me not to call anymore. I asked her how Shin was doing. "Fine, no thanks to you," she said. *No thanks to me?* If it wasn't for me, her son would have been struck by lightning. "His mom wouldn't let me talk to him," I say.

"I don't blame her. None of us should ever have listened to you. God is not a joke."

"Sounds like you've been talking to your old man."

"I just don't think you should joke about it."

"Are you forsaking the Ten-legged One?"

"Cut it out, Jason. You think you're being funny, but it's blasphemy."

"You really have been listening to your dad."

"So? If I'd listened to him instead of you, none of this would have happened."

"Is this about me hitting you with the ping-pong ball?"

He picks up his bag and poker. "Get lost, Jason." He stabs the muskrat with his poker, stuffs it into his bag, and walks away.

Maybe I'm the Antichrist. Maybe I'm a pawn of Satan. But I don't *feel* evil. Besides, if God is real, what does he care about some kid from St. Andrew Valley worshipping a water tower? When I die, do I go straight to hell—or just serve a few millennia in purgatory? I'll have to ask Just Al about that. It's the sort of thing he would have an opinion on.

Maybe Dan is right, and it's my fault that he's picking up dead muskrats, and that Henry busted his leg, and that Shin got hauled off to the psych ward. But if I'd never invented Chutengodianism, things might have been worse. Maybe Shin's snails would have started talking to him, or the voice of Zolag, Uber King of Nutbagia, would have come to him through his shoelaces. Maybe Henry would have fallen off the tower and died. Who knows? Things *could* be worse.

Still, I keep hearing my father's voice: *Your friends listen to what you say.*

I wait down the street from Shin's house until I see Mrs. Schinner get in her car and drive off, probably to run some errands. As soon as she's out of sight, I run around to the back and knock on Shin's window. No response. The side door is unlocked; I let myself in.

Shin is lying on his unmade bed in his X-men pajamas, sleeping.

I look around. Dirty clothes scattered across the floor. Walls covered with maps and drawings and posters. Shelves jammed with computer games and comic books and books about snails and trains and astronomy and math puzzles and chess—all of Shin's nerdy passions. Desk piled high with more books and coffee cans full of technical pens and mechanical pencils and colored markers and, in the center of it, a large spiral-bound sketchbook. In short, everything looks like before, with one glaring exception.

The gastropodarium is missing.

I watch Shin sleep. His breathing is choppy. His spidery fingers curl and twitch, and I can see his eyes moving beneath closed eyelids. Dreaming. I am afraid to wake him up. I am afraid he will not be the Shin I know. Was Dan right? Has Shin really gone off the deep end?

I sit down at his desk and open the sketchbook. Page after page is covered from edge to edge with his crabbed script. I start reading in the middle of the page.

. . . and I saw ten thousand towers descend on pillars of flame and as they settled upon the plain their members did bore deep into the firmament and inject new life into the parched soil, and the towers did crumble then and give their substance unto the Earth . . .

I wonder if the men who wrote the Bible were anything like Shin. I turn the page. More writing. Thousands of words. More words than I have written in my entire life. I flip through the pages, not reading, just staring at the sheer mass of words.

About two-thirds of the way through the book, the words abruptly end:

. . . for it is by my image that you shall know me, and it is by my image that you shall be saved.

I turn the page to a drawing of the St. Andrew Valley water tower: The Ten-legged One in all his glory, with every strut, seam, cable, and rivet precisely and lovingly rendered with the tip of an ultra-fine technical pen, a masterpiece of accuracy and detail. It must have taken him hours. Maybe days. I turn to the next page, and the next. More towers. Not just water towers, but towers of every description. Some of them I recognize. The Eiffel Tower. The twin towers of the World Trade Center, before it collapsed. Others are fantasy towers, convoluted, ornate constructions. But most of the drawings are of water towers. Towers with double and triple tanks. Towers with tanks balanced on impossibly thin columns. Water towers in flight. I page through slowly, astonished by the quality, precision, and detail of the illustrations. I knew Shin could draw, but I never knew he could draw like this.

I am looking at a picture of a pair of distorted dark towers standing on a mountaintop when I feel Shin's breath on my neck.

I spin around in the chair.

"Hey," I say.

Shin's eyes are sleepy, his mouth is slack, his hair is sticking out all to one side.

He points at the dark towers. "My parents," he says.

"How are you doing?" I ask.

"I'm good." He turns the page. "This is me," he says.

The drawing is of a tall, spidery, insubstantial-looking tower.

"What happened to your pods?"

"My pods?" He smiles. "I let them all go. I let my pods go." He turns to a drawing of a tower with knotted, twisted legs and a distorted, angry-looking tank. "See this one? You know who this is?"

Oddly enough, I recognize it. "Is it Henry?"

"Right." He turns the page to a sleek and jaunty five-legged tower.

"Magda," I say.

He shows me more. Columns of towers representing the police; a great squat tank representing the St. Andrew Valley High School; a pallid, featureless tower that is unmistakably Dan Grant.

"Look," he says, turning the page to a large, blocky water tower supported by four stout columns. The drawing is larger than any of the others, filling the page from edge to edge. "That's you," he says.

I look at him, right in the eyes.

"Shin, are you crazy?"

"I don't know," he says. "Do you think I am?"

"Well, this water tower stuff . . . it seems like you're, you know, so *into* it. You don't really think the water tower is God, do you?"

His eyebrows crumple. "Don't you?"

"As a joke, sure. But . . . no, I don't."

He is looking at the sketchbook, at his rendering of Tower God Jason Bock.

"You said you did," he says.

"Yeah, but I was—"

"How do you know it's not true if you don't believe in it?"

"I . . . huh?"

He looks up from the sketchbook and into my eyes. "How can you understand something you don't believe in?"

"Shin, that doesn't make any sense. That's like saying you can't understand leprechauns unless you believe in them."

"Do you understand leprechauns?"

"I don't believe in them."

"There you go."

A<small>ND IN THE END, ONLY THE</small> O<small>CEAN REMAINED,</small>
A<small>ND THE</small> O<small>CEAN WAS ALONE.</small>

31

I met with my father the other day

to give him my book reports. The meeting got off to a rough start when I told him that I had written nothing.

"Here's my report," I said, empty-handed. "I didn't care for any of them."

He stares at me, his face showing nothing. "You read them all?"

"I read as much as I could. They're all pretty much the same."

"Oh? You're telling me that *Teen Jesus* is indistinguishable from Thomas Merton's *The Seven Storey Mountain*?"

"They all require a belief in a supreme being. If you don't believe in God, then the books don't mean much."

My father sighed and sat back and said, "You think you're an atheist, then?"

"I'm not sure what I am."

He looked at me for a long time then. I think it was the longest time he has ever looked at me without saying anything. Finally, he spoke.

"I'm sorry to hear that, Jason."

"Why?"

"Because it means you've got a long, lonely road ahead of you."

"It's my road."

"You're right about that." His shoulders dropped and I felt something go out of him, as if he had been holding his breath for years and had suddenly remembered to exhale.

"All right then," he said, his mouth curved into a sad smile. It wasn't one of his usual looks—angry, bewildered, impatient, friendly, curious, or astonished. It was more of a *level* look, a look of recognition and understanding.

"All right then . . . what?" I asked.

"You're sixteen, old enough to make your own choices. I'm not going to force anything on you. If you don't want to go to church anymore, that's up to you. TPO meetings are optional. Worship water towers, trees, frogs, whatever."

"What's the catch?"

He laughed, shaking his head. "There are a lot of perfectly good religions out there. You're a smart kid, Jason. I know you'll find what you're looking for."

✳ ✳ ✳

One week before school starts I am at Crossroads Mall to buy myself a new pair of shoes—I wore out my last pair out on Route 17. I am hulking along the mezzanine, imagining myself as a mountain troll from Middle Earth, when I see Henry and Magda. Henry is still on crutches. Magda is walking with him, talking and laughing, carrying two shopping bags in one hand and touching his arm with the other. I stop and watch them approach. They are so wrapped up in each other they don't notice me until they are about to crash right into me.

"Jay-boy!" Henry says. "What are you doing here? I thought you were grounded for the next ten years."

"They let me out," I say, feeling excessively surly and trollish.

"Hi, Jason," Magda says, her face carefully composed.

I ignore her.

"Haven't seen any graffiti on the water tower lately," I say to Henry. "Was spelling out all those words too hard for your stooges?"

"Nah, but after your buddy Schinner tried to drown himself they put some motion detectors on the tower. We haven't figured out how to get past 'em, but we will. Soon as this thing—" He raps his plastic splint with a crutch. "—comes off."

Looking down at Henry, I wonder what Magda can possibly see in this skinny little guy on crutches. He can't even go shopping without a girl to carry his bags. I can hardly believe that, just a few weeks ago, I was afraid of him. There are plenty of scarier things in this world than Henry Stagg's knobby fists, especially to an oversize, leather-skinned mountain troll such as myself.

I look at him and laugh.

"What's so funny?" he says suspiciously.

"You are," I say, feeling reckless and angry. I turn to Magda and put an extra dash of nasty in my voice. "Haven't seen you at TPO lately." I had gone to the last three TPO meetings, mostly in hopes of seeing Magda, but she never showed up. Avoiding me, probably. Do I take it personally? Hell, yes.

"I've been busy," she says.

"Busy with *Henry*?"

"That is none of your business," she says, her big eyes becoming slits.

I look at Henry, who is scowling dangerously, then back at Magda.

"You could do better," I say, jerking my thumb in Henry's direction.

I see Henry's right arm move, but he's too fast for me. His crutch whacks me across the side of my head and I go down like a 230-pound sack of lard. Next thing I know I'm staring up at Henry Stagg's flushed, knotted features, and above him the bright white fluorescent light fixtures are spinning and I hear Magda's voice crying, "Omigod! Omigod!"

They're keeping me overnight in the hospital because I

have a mild concussion from my head hitting the floor. It took seven stitches to sew my scalp back together, which will leave a really interesting scar. My mother is hysterical, of course. My father wants to press charges. Henry is banished forever from Crossroads Mall. And Magda sent me a bunch of flowers and a get well card.

Yeah, my head hurts right now, but as Henry might say, "You live to be a hundred, you're gonna remember it like it was yesterday."

The middle of the night in a hospital is a good time to think. It's mostly quiet (except for the constant beeping of machines, and the occasional death rattle) and there is nothing to do *but* think. So I've been thinking about Shin, remembering what he said to me last time I saw him—that you can't really understand something until you believe in it. It sounded crazy to me at the time, but the more I think about it, the more it makes sense. For example, you can't really understand what it means to be Catholic (or Muslim, or whatever) unless you have faith. And you can't understand algebra unless you believe in numbers. Same deal with gastropods and water towers.

Maybe Shin's got it right. He just decides to believe in something, then he dives right in. I suppose in a few weeks he'll get rid of the water tower obsession just as he got rid of his snails, and move on to something new. Leprechauns, maybe. Does that make him crazy? I don't know. In a way I envy him. He always seems to know what he wants.

I envy my father, too. I envy his unshakable belief in the Catholic Church—his faith gives him power and contentment. I envy everyone who has a religion they can believe in. I envy Henry and Magda, who believe in each other. I even envy Dan, who thinks I'm a dangerous heretic.

Me? I have Chutengodianism—a religion with no church, no money, and only one member. I have a religion, but I have no faith. Maybe one day I'll find a deity I can believe in. Until then, my god is made of steel and rust.